WEST END SYNAGOGUE
LIBRARY

Donated to
THE WEST END SYNAGOGUE
... by ...

MR. & MRS. LESTER S_LIN

IN MEMORY OF

ISADORE RAPOPORT

6550

*Here's to Your Health,
Comrade Shifrin!*

Here's to Your Health, Comrade Shifrin!

ILYA SUSLOV

Translated by Maxine Bronstein

Foreword by Maurice Friedberg

INDIANA UNIVERSITY PRESS / BLOOMINGTON & LONDON

Copyright © 1977 by Indiana University Press
All rights reserved
No part of this book may be reproduced or utilized in any form or by any means, electronic or mechanical, including photocopying and recording, or by any information storage and retrieval system, without permission in writing from the publisher. The Association of American University Presses' Resolution on Permissions constitutes the only exception to this prohibition.
Published in Canada by Fitzhenry & Whiteside Limited, Don Mills, Ontario
Manufactured in the United States of America

Library of Congress Cataloging in Publication Data

Suslov, Il'iā Petrovich.
   Here's to your health, Comrade Shifrin!

   I. Title.
PZ4.S9599He3 [PG3488.U73] 891.7'4'4 76-26422
ISBN 0-253-13710-1 1 2 3 4 5 81 80 79 78 77

Foreword

Foreword

IN THE USSR, laughter is no joking matter. A disrespectful quip may still, even in these more enlightened post-Stalin days, result in a prison sentence as malicious propaganda. And conversely, even Soviet circus clowns are organized into a stodgy union, complete with committees, congresses, and dreary speeches exhorting the funny-men not to lose sight of the *political* importance of their work. It goes without saying that the authorities supervise even more closely the authors of comic prose, verse, and drama.

In 1952, on the occasion of the centennial of Gogol's death, an appeal to the Soviet literary community was issued by Georgi Malenkov, then one of Stalin's closest associates. Soviet writers were informed of the country's pressing need for humorists and satirists, and were called upon to produce "Soviet Gogols and Saltykov-Shchedrins." That the need was indeed very real was obvious to all. Two decades of ruthless regimentation of literature and the arts had wrought devastation in many genres of writing. Yet nowhere was the desolation as complete as in the area of humor and satire. The country's lone Russian satirical journal, *Krokodil,* most often mocked the bourgeois West—and particularly

Foreword

the United States—but its tone was far too shrill and its didactic purposes too transparent to be at all amusing. *Krokodil* would also occasionally gently rap the knuckles of a minor Soviet bureaucrat or an inefficient salesman in a government-owned store. Even politics aside, none of this was very funny. In essence, Soviet humor and satire of the last years of Stalin's life bore much resemblance to a movie cartoon that mocks mythical foreign beasts never seen by the audience, or else chastizes helpless mice for running from the glorious, noble cat. As if to dramatize this state of affairs, the most important living comic writer, Mikhail Zoshchenko, whose reputation was made in earlier, more permissive times, was publicly excommunicated in 1946 and expelled from the Union of Soviet Writers for his irreverence toward official pieties—for a satirist, an inevitable professional hazard. The other famous Soviet comic writers, Ilya Ilf and Yevgeni Petrov, had both died some years earlier. Still, the wrath of the Establishment was to be visited on their books. *The Twelve Chairs* and *The Little Golden Calf*, both of them innocent enough romps describing the misadventures of a Soviet crook and confidence man and both read to shreds by generations of Soviet citizens, were never banned outright, but they were not reprinted either. Even these authors' *One-Storied America* fell into disfavor. Its often pointed barbs at the United States were thought to be too gentle and hence incompatible with the tone of anti-American hysteria obligatory in Soviet writing and journalism of the Cold War era.

At the time of Stalin's death in 1953, hardly any comic writing was being produced. The short-lived periods of liberalization that followed, in 1956 and again in 1962, engendered disappointingly little original comic literature. True, the timid Soviet humorist Leonid Lench may have become a bit more outspoken, and the comic stage monologues of Arkadi Raikin may have become

Foreword

enlivened with more pointed material. Still, by and large, the major beneficiaries of the more permissive atmosphere were to be the old books that had been earlier neglected or suppressed. Thus, after an interval of over two decades, Soviet theaters began to perform once again the two comedies by Vladimir Mayakovsky, *The Bedbug* and *The Bathhouse*. (There was some irony here because the comedies were considered taboo at a time when Mayakovsky's propagandistic verse was memorized by millions of schoolchildren.) Relaxation of controls encouraged the revival of Alexander Sukhovo-Kobylin, the nineteenth-century dramatist whose pointedly satirical attacks on the corrupt tsarist bureaucracy and, more daringly, police, could now be seen on the Soviet stage. The "thaw" benefited even two émigré Russian humorists with established reputations in prerevolutionary Russia, Nadezhda Teffi and Arkadi Averchenko—both, to be sure, deceased. Bookstores began to display reprints of Ilf and Petrov as well as Zoshchenko (true, only in bowdlerized versions), and also the brilliantly ironic tales of Isaac Babel, just then posthumously "rehabilitated" after more than two decades as a literary unperson. Among books reissued was an early satirical novel by an author whose many years of devoted service as Stalinist apologist made him now the more eager to champion the liberal cause. Ilya Ehrenburg's *Julio Jurenito* was included in a multivolume set of his collected works, although his other picaresque work, *Lazik Roitschwantz*, was not—by Ehrenburg's own admission, because of its Jewish subject matter. That the comic tradition in Russian writing was not wholly destroyed during the Stalin era, and that at least some had simply gone underground, was attested by one of the most remarkable literary excavations in the history of modern writing. Mikhail Bulgakov, who at the time of his death in 1940 was known only as the author of the remarkable novel with

ix

Foreword

a Civil War setting, *The White Guard,* as well as several plays and stage adaptations, emerged in the 1960s as the foremost Russian comic writer of this century. He earned this new distinction posthumously, not through the normal process of a reappraisal of his reputation, but as a result of publication of previously unknown works. Bulgakov's *The Master and Margarita,* which blends an unconventional retelling of the life of Christ with a story of the Devil's adventures in Stalin's Moscow, contains many pages of first-rate comic prose. *Theatrical Novel* (published in English under the title *The Black Snow*) is a magnificently irreverent lampoon of Konstantin Stanislavsky, a sacred cow of the Russian and world theater. Finally, there was the short novel, *The Heart of a Dog,* a brilliant satire on the presumptions of science and, by extension, of social engineering itself. Because of its understandable ideological sensitivity, the latter novel, unlike the others, was not published in the Soviet Union, and appeared only abroad. Also, the two post-Stalin decades saw a large influx into the USSR of Western European and American literature, including much comic writing.

Still, of original new Russian comic and satirical prose, drama, and verse there was precious little, a sign perhaps of the precarious nature of the post-Stalin liberalization in the arts. It is therefore significant that much comic writing has appeared only surreptitiously in the body of literature now universally known as *samizdat* and in the equally illegal tape recordings called *magnitizdat.* In the sixties and early seventies the satirical songs of Alexander Galich (who now lives in Western Europe) and of Vladimir Vysotsky, with their sentimental bittersweet mockery of the absurdities of Soviet existence, provided a degree of catharsis at countless social gatherings in Russia's overcrowded apartments. Incongruities of Soviet conventions and pretenses, which fit well Henri Bergson's definition of

Foreword

the comic as "something mechanical encrusted upon the living," also inspired the first satirical works of *samizdat* that reached the West in the early 1960s, those of "Abram Tertz" and "Nikolai Arzhak." The satirical effectiveness of these authors' efforts was largely a result of their irreverence with respect not only to official values, but even to those of their fellow-nonconformists. Thus, one of Tertz's stories advanced a brilliantly unorthodox thesis about censorship's deadening impact on literature. Instead of the usual claim that such controls stifle the appearance of much talented work that happens to be politically unorthodox, the story suggested that unacknowledged but all-too-real political censorship serves as a convenient excuse for graphomania, with rejection slips displayed proudly as badges of courage. At the two authors' trial early in 1966, when their true identities were revealed (Tertz was Andrei Sinyavsky, and Arzhak was the pen name of Yuli Daniel), the varying degrees of intensity of the prosecution's wrath helped establish a hierarchy of sorts of subjects that are considered sensitive in Soviet literature. One must not, except with the greatest circumspection, discuss the problem of police controls. Nothing but hushed reverence will do when Lenin's name is mentioned (Daniel's somewhat clumsy *This is Moscow Speaking*, in which the image of Lenin was conjured up, of all times, during sexual intercourse, understandably enraged the staid Soviet judges). And the subject of Jews (let alone of state-condoned Soviet anti-Semitism) was, it was emphasized, off limits. That Sinyavsky, a pure Russian, chose the Jewish pseudonym Abram Tertz was viewed by the Moscow court as a vicious provocation. The prosecutor called it an attempt to insinuate that in the Soviet Socialist state there actually exists a Jewish problem: as any reader of Soviet newspapers ought to know, the abomination of anti-Semitism can exist only in capitalist conditions, in

xi

Foreword

such countries as America, old Nazi and neo-Nazi Germany, and (yes, especially!) in Israel.

In the decade that followed, the themes of *samizdat* and new émigré Russian writing confirmed the list of taboos implied at Sinyavsky's and Daniel's trial. That most of this literature dealt with the subject of prison camps (it is the central concern of all but one of Solzhenitsyn's novels) comes as no surprise, and the subject is hardly conducive to laughter. (There is, to be sure, one successful *Soviet* comedy about concentration camps, Nikolai Pogodin's *Aristocrats*.) The other taboos, however, have inspired illegal writing in the comic vein. There are the stories of Yuri Krotkov about the sexual exploits of the late Soviet secret police chief Lavrenti Beria—a subject that is offensive on both political and "moral" grounds. There is *Vanya Chmotanov,* an anonymous *samizdat* novella about the theft of Lenin's head from his embalmed corpse in the mausoleum in Moscow's Red Square by a petty crook who believes, not unreasonably, that anything so closely guarded must be of great value, perhaps to Western intelligence. There are the pathetic and funny tales of Efraim Sevela about Jewish survivors of the Holocaust in a country rife with Jew-hatred, where one cannot even complain because, officially, Jews are equal to others and must therefore be happy. And finally, there is the delightful burlesque of Soviet military brass and the secret police, *The Life of Ivan Chonkin*. Although the novel has appeared so far only abroad, its author, Vladimir Voinovich, lives in the USSR.

It is against the background of these traditions that Ilya Suslov's novel must be viewed. There are echoes of Yiddish anecdotes in it, anecdotes that for many years (together with their main competition, the Armenian ones) served as Soviet Russia's most important uncensored quasi-literary commentary on the affairs of state and their impact on the human condition. So great has

Foreword

been their role that Sinyavsky, who now lives in the West, has suggested that these anecdotes will nourish future Russian literature much as folklore inspired Pushkin's verse. As for literary influences, most readily discernible are those of the Odessa school of comic writing, of Isaac Babel and of Ilf and Petrov. All three, of course, had themselves been raised on Yiddish anecdotes, were never entirely weaned, and for the rest of their lives retained an addiction to their irony and sadness. It was these anecdotes that imparted the melancholy knowledge of Ecclesiastes that nothing is really new under the sun, that human nature is least likely to change, that most often new labels disguise old problems, and that *hubris* is but a fancy word for familiar *chutzpa*. From Ilf and Petrov, whose work Ilya Suslov greatly admires (during his tenure at the Moscow newspaper *Literaturnaya gazeta* he supervised the humor column, entitled "The Twelve Chairs Club"), the book borrows some of the mannerisms of Ostap Bender, their picaresque hero, although the bureaucrats whom Suslov's Tolya Shifrin must battle are infinitely more menacing than Ilf and Petrov's fumbling provincial officials. The influence of Babel is much in evidence throughout, and not only in the Yiddishisms of Abram Moiseyevich in the hospital (the old man who undergoes an eminently successful operation and dies immediately thereafter) or of Lev Yakovlevich, the boss of the printing shop who, in order to escape a *certain* prison sentence, constantly cheats the state, thus only *risking* prison. That type of lexicon and syntax is now familiar to American readers from the books of Philip Roth and Bernard Malamud, whose protagonists converse in its English equivalent. The impact of Babel is felt, more importantly, in the succinct, polished, somewhat nervous narrative and, above all, in an obvious effort to avoid melodrama and to relate stories of blatant injustice (which, viewed by the young Tolya Shif-

Foreword

rin, assume the dimensions of real tragedy) with detachment and irony. It is for that reason, perhaps, that we are never introduced to Tolya Shifrin's family: it would have been difficult for an adolescent hero to sustain this posture. Sentimentality does break through, however, in the chapter relating Tolya's trip to Georgia, the beautiful land in the Caucasus that has traditionally captivated Russian poets, who surrounded it with a romantic halo, much as Italy enchanted their German and British counterparts.

As we follow Tolya Shifrin on his journey from high school, through college and a stint in the printing shop and in the publishing house, to his final position as a member of the editorial staff of a major Soviet newspaper (all of them based on the author's experiences in real life), we are introduced to a gallery of human types who also represent a variety of responses to the demands of the state. We look at schoolteachers whose pupils brazenly parrot newspaper slogans on examinations knowing that one cannot be flunked for voicing *correct* opinions—but who also attempt to imbue in their pupils a love for good literature. We observe workers in the printing shop on the verge of a strike when the bosses—that is, the State—impose on them higher production quotas. We meet their overseers charged with implementing those quotas which, incongruously, cannot be met without actually breaking the law. Together with Tolya, sent as a student to help out with the harvest, we listen to the gruesome life story of a Russian peasant who, as a result of persecutions, has lost all taste for farming. We observe people who roll with the punches—the factory bosses, the editors, and even Party organizers. Though fully aware of the injustice and senselessness of policies they implement, they cynically toe the line. We make the acquaintance of two men who donned their country's uniform not to defend their homeland from foreign enemies but to

Foreword

wage war on their own people. The first, once an army officer and now a pitiful drunkard, was, as it turns out, decorated for his "noble" role in the deportation of peaceful Soviet citizens. The other, a former border guard celebrated in Soviet films, did not, as the films suggested, protect Soviet frontiers from infiltration by foreign spies and saboteurs; his real task was to prevent the escape abroad of inmates of Gulag Archipelago. And lest we believe that distrust and informing and fear of Soviet police are all but a memory of the tragic Stalin era, we meet two Party goons sent to spy on a group of Soviet citizens on a visit to—of all places!—Bulgaria, not only a Communist country, but traditionally pro-Russian as well.

All of these episodes highlight individual ills of Soviet society, and even though Suslov's generally lighthearted narration is a far cry from Solzhenitsyn's impassioned denunciations, most fall in the category of forbidden subjects that are hinted at only occasionally in officially sanctioned Soviet writing. One central theme, however innocent it may appear to a foreign reader, remains taboo. When we first meet Tolya Shifrin, we take him for an ordinary boy from Moscow, and doubtless he considers himself one. Before long, however, he begins to realize that he is different because he is a Jew. Although Tolya is Russian by culture and upbringing and conventionally Russian in his values and aspirations, his official documents—which in the USSR must be presented on countless occasions—identify him as a Jew. When, in spite of an impressive performance on the entrance examination, he is turned down by the faculty of journalism, he becomes suspicious. When the same thing happens in engineering, he threatens to complain to Comrade Stalin, who must surely be unaware of the illegal discrimination. Yet Tolya was clearly not alone, as attested by the crowds of boys and girls, displaying every conceivable proof of academic

Foreword

excellence but wearing eyeglasses, the symbol of Jewishness made famous by Isaac Babel. Later, he stands ready to enter a naval academy (it *is* higher education, isn't it?) when the military officer discovers to his horror that Shifrin's papers identify him as a Jew. The officer, however, remains quite ready to draft him as a private. (Curiously, an analogous tale was told at the turn of the century by the great Yiddish humorist Sholom Aleichem. The setting was tsarist Russia, where anti-Semitic discrimination was openly acknowledged.) And when, by a fluke, Tolya is admitted to college and thus escapes the draft, the Soviet officer expresses his wonder: wouldn't you know, the Jews always find a way out!

The growth of Tolya's ethnic consciousness is portrayed as gradual and rooted in a progression of events that spans the period from Stalin's declining years through the early 1970s. The first incident that awakens Tolya's awareness of his Jewishness is the 1952 Doctors' Plot, when a group of Soviet physicians, most of them Jewish, were accused of plotting the medical murder of Soviet leaders. Suslov shows only the fright of an old news-vendor and a glimpse of the orgy of anti-Semitic hatred in college, but these are sufficient. Another event is the carefully orchestrated denunciation of Israel by prominent Soviet Jews in the wake of the Six-Day War of 1967. Neither experience made Tolya yearn for Zion, but they confirmed him in a sense of ethnic self-respect. Tolya Shifrin's Jewishness is clearly of the kind defined by Jean-Paul Sartre: a Jew is one whom others consider a Jew. Much the same is suggested by the grotesque account of the wedding of Tolya's friend and a young woman whose socially very prominent background is soiled by her biological origins. Though a descendant of a famous Civil War hero, she is also partly Jewish.

At the end of Ilya Suslov's book, five "reader's reports" illustrate different Soviet views of the proper

Foreword

function of literature. The first is quite simple: write what the Party wants you to write, "the truth is what the people and the Party respect." Interestingly, this reader retains warm memories of SS-men, prisoners of war in Siberia. And he advises Tolya to use his writing talent in a way that will earn him material rewards. The second reader says much the same thing, but in far more sophisticated terms: literature should inspire people for heroic deeds or, at the very least, serve as harmless entertainment. The third, the wife of a career Party bureaucrat, regrets that the book devotes little attention to love and, significantly if not entirely *a propos*, complains about the bitter clashes between her Stalinist husband and "liberal" son, a situation reminiscent of two of *samizdat*'s most important novels: Tertz's *The Trial Begins* and Solzhenitsyn's *Cancer Ward*. The fourth, a war veteran who also spent some time in Soviet camps, complains about the naiveté of the young generation. Finally, the fifth, a Jew, implies that the book is pretty much irrelevant, that one must leave the USSR because the Soviet system is incapable of reform and, besides, a revolution would result in a massacre of intellectuals and, of course, of the Jews. Emigration is thus the only answer, even though the émigrés, of whatever ethnic stock, will never cease being Russian.

In an important essay entitled "The Literary Process in Russia," which appeared in 1974 in the inaugural issue of *Kontinent,* a Russian journal published in the West, Andrei Sinyavsky, who retains his Jewish pseudonym Abram Tertz, pointed to some major links between the Jewish problem in the USSR and Russian literature:

> First of all, the Jewish problem is linked most directly and intimately to the literary process—because every Russian writer (of Russian [non-Jewish] origin) who does not wish to write as he is told is a Jew. He is an outcast and an enemy

xvii

Foreword

of the people. . . . Second, the present Jewish Exodus from Russia overlaps to a large extent with the departure of manuscripts from Russia. Just think of those manuscripts crossing the frontier. Every one of them is taking risks. Every one of them was registered in advance in a list of those that must be destroyed because they are Yids, because they are in the way.

Andrei Sinyavsky's essay ends with a vision of a set of Saltykov-Shchedrin's books fleeing Russia while there is still time. The great satirist's numerous traveling companions clearly include the life story of Tolya Shifrin, a Jewish kid from Moscow.

University of Illinois at Urbana-Champaign   MAURICE FRIEDBERG

Here's to Your Health, Comrade Shifrin!

―――――――――――――――――――――*1*

I GOT A STOMACH ACHE. At first I ignored it. I thought it was something I ate. And then suddenly something burst inside me, and the pain welled to the surface.
"Where does it hurt, Tolik?" my mother asked anxiously.
"Ow, everywhere; ow, it hurts," I groaned.
An ambulance came right away. "It looks like appendicitis," said the doctor, and off we went on a chase all over Moscow in search of an empty hospital bed. The doctor swore. "No room," they told him everywhere. Finally, he deposited me in some hospital way out in Sokolniki and said with relief, "Get better, kid."
I lay in the corridor, pressing my hands against the pain in my right side and thinking about what would happen in school the next day. Maria Vladimirovna would mark who was present in her class register.
"He's not here!" Marik Khazanov, my deskmate, would crow.
"Where is he?" Maria Vladimirovna would ask sternly.
Marik would piously roll his eyes and shrug his shoulders helplessly.
"Stop fooling around, Khazanov," Maria Vladimi-

3

Here's to Your Health,

rovna would say. "Maybe your friend is sick, and here you are making faces. You'd better find out what happened to Tolik."

Marik would say, "Maria Vladimirovna, let me run over to his house and see. Maybe something happened to him. Maybe his aunt got sick."

"Only make it quick," Maria Vladimirovna would say. (She likes me and worries about me.) And Marik would wink at Vovka Mulin, grab his cap, and run to the Perekop movie theater to see *The Fate of a Soldier in America.*

"What a rat!" I thought, gritting my teeth. "Here I lie dying of appendicitis, and he's running to the movies." Some friend! To tell the truth, in his place I would have done the same thing, but at the moment I was very hurt.

It was dark in the corridor where I lay. I could sense that the place was crammed with beds. Everywhere people were groaning, gasping, snoring. Then the ceiling began to cave in on me, the light bulb in the corner became large and iridescent. It burned brighter, brighter . . . I screamed.

Someone came over, felt my stomach, and said, "On the operating table—right away!"

They put me on a white cart and wheeled me to the operating room.

I was terribly embarrassed. There I lay naked in front of three girls my age.

I whispered to one of them, "Let's go to the movies after the operation." She said, "Lie still. A big-mouth, you are. We'll cut off your you-know-what; later you'll be going to the movies without us." The girls giggled.

"Big deal, she puts on a hospital gown, and now she's a big shot."

A woman doctor entered and said, "Who's this talkative character? Young man, in your condition you don't make dates with girls."

Comrade Shifrin!

While she spoke, they gave me an injection. Suddenly I was afraid I would die right there. "Doctor, bury me in Red Square."

"Bite your tongue, you idiot," said the doctor, and she stuck me in the stomach with something cold and hard. I lost consciousness. . . .

"Well, you're a regular hero!" The doctor patted me on the cheek. "If you had come to the hospital ten minutes later, we would have had one less chatterbox in the world. Just look what we've cut out of you."

"My God!" I cried. "What a lot of crap a person has inside him! Who needs appendicitis?"

"You talk too much," the doctor said sternly. "Another Spinoza I have here. Take him to the ward; let him rest. Next!"

Our ward was large. We lay there after our operations and moaned as the anesthetic wore off; we were in pain.

It must have been a funny sight.

My neighbor to the right set the pitch for us all.

"O-o-o-o!" he howled ever so delicately in a falsetto.

"Ookh!" someone in the right-hand corner exhaled.

"M-m-m!" I mooed next.

"Ah-kh!" My neighbor on the left picked up the baton in this relay race in a weak basso voice.

A regular Piatnitsky Chorus!

Towards morning things quieted down. Exhausted from lack of sleep, we looked around to see who our neighbors were.

Professor Dunayevsky was making the morning rounds. They said that he was the brother of the famous Soviet composer of military marches. He began at the bed of my right-hand neighbor.

"Well, old man," he said, looking over the hospital chart and feeling the patient's pulse. "How long do you intend to make my life miserable? You exasperate me, you old devil."

"Excuse me, Professor, said the old man on my right. "You're a smart man, and you know how hard it is to make up your mind to have such an operation. I have to consult with my relatives."

"Abram Moiseyevich!" thundered the professor. "Don't give me that. You've been consulting with your relatives for a month now. I will operate on you myself. What are you afraid of? One, two, three, and it will be all over. Well?"

"Ah, Professor," said the old man on my right. "Put yourself in my place. I'm an old, sick man. I'm seventy-eight years old. When you get to be my age, I'd like to see how easily you'll be deciding these vital questions. I've called Rivochka from Dnepropetrovsk. Whatever she says, that's what I'll do. All right?"

"Blankety-blank!" trumpeted Professor Dunayevsky. "All right, we'll wait for Rivochka."

"Grandpa," I said when the professor had left our ward, surrounded by assistants and nurses. "Grandpa, if they haven't operated on you yet, then why were you groaning all night as if they had cut you up and down?"

"Okh!" said Abram Moiseyevich. "Another critic I need! I was groaning because it hurt me to look at you. When they operate on me, you'll help me groan. Okay?"

If you ask me, Abram Moiseyevich really loved his ailment. He had a hernia. Every day he sent telegrams to cities all over the Soviet Union and abroad. Since all his relatives knew about the hernia, he simply wrote, "To do or not to do. Stop. Abram Moiseyevich."

Answers were cabled from all corners of the world. He sorted them into three piles. In one pile he put the "To do" telegrams; in the second pile went the "Not to do"s. The third pile consisted of vague responses: "Do as you like," "I don't know," "I should only have your troubles," "Abram, don't lose your head." These telegrams Abram Moiseyevich did not like. "Look, Tolik,"

Comrade Shifrin!

he said, "what kind of indifferent people there are in the world. These aren't people, they're animals. An old sick uncle consults them on a question of life or death. What does it cost them to say "yes." Or "no." They should be ashamed to spend money on such idiotic answers. Tolik, you should love people and not love nonpeople. You get me?"

My neighbor on the left was the same age as Abram Moiseyevich. Abram Moiseyevich had no respect for him. "He's a dirty old man," he whispered to me. "You shouldn't associate with him, Tolik. He's a relic of capitalism."

"Why do you talk that way about him, Abram Moiseyevich?"

"Okh!" said Abram Moiseyevich. "What kind of a man can he be if all he thinks about is women?"

I peered cautiously at my neighbor on the left. He was an absolutely dry ruin of a man. He was passive and quiet. There was something wrong with his bladder.

Every other day his wife visited him. She was a small, neat old woman. "Mashenka, my pussycat," my left-hand neighbor lisped each time, greeting his wife. She sat down next to him on the edge of the bed and fed him something sweet from a spoon. Then they cooed, looking lovingly into each other's eyes. Then she would leave. It could make you envious.

"Mashenka is a darling, not a woman," lisped the old man on my left. "A saint. A heavenly angel."

I couldn't understand Abram Moiseyevich's hostility towards my neighbor.

"Just wait, he'll reveal himself yet!" whispered Abram Moiseyevich. "You don't know anything about people. That womanizer! Degenerate! Tfu! What slime!"

The old man on the left intrigued me terribly. I also wanted to be a degenerate then, but I hadn't yet been successful. When I went to parties with girls from the neighboring school, they considered me interesting. But all I had to do after dances was to lead them away somewhere into a corner on the fifth floor, and they would get scared and only let me kiss them. Yes, my neighbor on the left positively fascinated me!

"Ivan Vasilievich," I asked him, "what did you do before the Revolution?"

And the old man on my left told his story. Before the Revolution he had an "establishment" on Petrovka. . . .

He was completely transformed. His face blazed, his eyes burned with an inner light. He forgot about his bladder and reminisced, "Then, you know, I would order myself a little Spanish lady. Black hair, raven-colored, and how her eyes sparkled! Legs—wow! Breasts —a goddess! An exceptional woman. And I had sixteen of them, each one better than the next. I would look up, you know, and they would all say with respect, 'Welcome, Ivan Vasilievich!' A good-looker I was then. Velvet vest, with a chain, I had. A moustache, of course, a beard. . . . A real hero! A cavalier with the Order of Saint George! I would shout to make the windows rattle. Then I'd take Tamara, put her in the sleigh, cover her with a bear skin, and off we'd go!"

The old man on the left blazed up like a book of matches. He waved his arms, yelled, and jumped up and down on his bed. Abram Moiseyevich was too disgusted to even look at him. He said, "My dear dead Bertochka, may she rest in peace, always told me, 'Don't have anything to do with woman-chasers; they're the cause of all the misery in the world.' Bertochka was a smart woman. Now I see what she had in mind."

"Abram Moiseyevich," I said, "What about you? Didn't you know any women besides Bertochka, for whom I have only the highest respect?"

"What a question!" he exploded. "Of course not!

Comrade Shifrin!

Look at me, now look at this degenerate creature, and you'll understand how one should live."

I looked at both of them and decided that neither one would do.

"What's to be done?" I thought. "How is one to live? Here are two old men at the finish line, and which of them is right? I don't know . . ."

"You really shouldn't hear such talk," said Abram Moiseyevich. "You're still a baby. Citizen," he addressed Ivan Vasilievich, "I understand that contributing to the delinquency of minors is your profession, but don't forget that we're in a hospital, and that the Revolution, thank God, swept away your class."

"You're going too far." Ivan Vasilievich got angry. "Don't you talk about the Revolution, you old goat, it maybe made a human being out of me, see?"

"Aha!" Abram Moiseyevich whispered to me. "The grave straightens a hunchback . . ."

And he shouted at Ivan Vasilievich, "Tell me, you provincial Don Juan, where are they now, your Spanish girls and your horses? And what in the world would you do if your wife, who doesn't know what you are, didn't visit you in this hospital? And what have you accomplished in your life altogether?"

"Don't you insult me!" screamed Ivan Vasilievich. "At least I have something to remember. And you, what have you done? What makes you so good? You're a tailor, that's what you are. Imagine, he thinks he's an air force hero! . . ."

"See that, Tolik?" said Abram Moiseyevich. "This man doesn't understand the meaning of life. He thinks he has insulted me. Of course I'm a tailor. But what a tailor! When a man puts on my jacket, you can right away send him to the London Exposition. And I have children. Do you know what it means to have children, you dirty old man?"

Abram Moiseyevich took out his telegrams and read,

Here's to Your Health,

" 'Do it.' That's from Yasha. When he was seven years old, he went off to America to join the Indians. He got on a train to leave for America, and Bertochka and I took him off the train. Do you know what it is to take your child off a train? Now he's a doctor. A doctor of mathematics. Let somebody tell me that Abram Moiseyevich shouldn't take off his child from a train so he can become a doctor!"

" 'Think about it. Stop. Misha.' "

"What do you think, you dirty old man, can a child write 'Think about it' if he himself has never once thought about anything? They told him 'it's necessary,' and he never thought 'necessary' or 'unnecessary.' 'Necessary' it was, and so off he went to Magnitogorsk, and Donbass, and Komsomolsk, and the devil knows where. Ten times I could tell him 'no,' but once he said 'yes' and left, and built, and suffered, and came back overgrown and said, 'There's a good life out there, Papa.' And if Misha writes 'Think about it' today, that means something's gone wrong. That means they've gotten to Misha. When the Germans tore off his arm during the war, he said, 'Thanks for not taking the other one. While I still have the other one, I'm still good for something, I'm still needed.'

"And such a boy writes 'Think about it.' Do you understand?

"And do you think that Rivochka is simply Rivochka? No, she's the mother of my grandsons! And you think raising such grandsons is easy? Just try raising such a Tolik, try taking all the rubbish out of his head so he'll learn to think, and not be afraid, and be a *mensch!* And all that at once! So, that's it, old man, life isn't so simple. And I haven't seen Rivochka's children yet. I must see them, then I can rest easy. These are my roots, you dirty old man . . ."

I was sick and tired of both of them. I began to occupy myself with the other patients.

Comrade Shifrin!
Once they brought into our ward some being wrapped from head to foot in bandages. The being snored with terrifying force. Only an atomic blast over his ear could have awakened him.
"What is this?" Abram Moiseyevich was horrified.
"He fell under a car," the attendant informed us.
"Why does he snore like that?"
"He hasn't sobered up yet . . ."
It was impossible to sleep with this terrifying roar. We decided to wait for our neighbor to wake up and find out what was going on in the outside world.
In the morning he told us:
"Well, you know, it was payday. Me and two other boys got together, you know. Well, then, we had another round. Well, then we left. And along comes a truck—vroom! I look, I think the truck has passed, and I start walking, see? And he's got a trailer, the bastard. I look around, and—bam!—I'm between the cab and the trailer. Well, you know, he's dragging me back and forth, up and down, and I'm yelling, 'Stop, I say!' and he's gone. They put twelve stitches in me. Let's the three of us buy a bottle. I'm getting out of here . . ."
My appendectomy was healing. I could already wander around the ward, holding my side. In place of the guy who fell under the truck, they sent us another. (Our mate, having withstood mutilation, could stand sobriety no longer, and during the night he unbandaged his wounds and fled. His soul was aflame, and he couldn't do without his pint of booze. He had absolutely terrified Abram Moiseyevich, who was on his account ready to decide for the operation. It was really a shame that the guy ran away.)
Professor Dunayevsky was getting really angry at Abram Moiseyevich. He was taking up someone else's place in the hospital. Abram Moiseyevich neatly spread out his miserable telegrams. Rivochka from Dnepropetrovsk arrived and said, "Do it." Then some wise-guy

from Malakhovka wrote, "Don't do it."

During the night Abram Moiseyevich awakened me and began to whisper, "Tolik, let's do it like this. On one piece of paper you'll write the word 'yes' and another piece of paper you'll leave blank. You'll fold the two pieces of paper and I'll pick one. If I pick 'yes,' then it'll be 'yes.' What else can I do?"

"Well," I thought, "all right, you old devil, I'll fix you." I took two scraps of paper, wrote the word 'yes' on both of them, folded them up, shook them around in my hands, and extended them towards the innocent Abram Moiseyevich.

He picked out a scrap of paper, saw his 'yes,' sighed, and fell silent.

I dropped off to sleep without a further thought.

In the morning Professor Dunayevsky stuck his head in the door and looked angrily at old Abram Moiseyevich.

"Professor," said my right-hand neighbor, "I say 'yes.' I say do it."

"Congratulations," said the professor. "We've crossed the Rubicon."

"What are you so happy about?" Abram Moiseyevich said mournfully. " 'You measure seven times, but you only cut once.' "

A white cart arrived, the old man was respectfully loaded on, and they wheeled it away. The patients silently sang the national anthem.

Abram Moiseyevich waved to us weakly as he was wheeled out the door.

An hour passed. Another. A third. The old man did not return.

"Auntie Klava," I yelled to the attendant in the corridor. "Give us the next; our Moiseyevich probably kicked the bucket. Give us a young one, it'll be merrier!"

Comrade Shifrin!

"Who are you to be giving orders, Tolik?" a familiar voice rang out from behind the door. "I'll show you a young one! Don't you dare take my place away!"

"Mother in heaven," Ivan Vasilievich crossed himself. "Look at that—Abram, he's come back alive. He's a live one, damned old devil."

"Hey, what took you so long, Abram Moiseyevich?" I asked. "We were getting all sorts of ideas . . . Was it a long operation?"

"Seven minutes," Abram Moiseyevich said proudly. "That professor is a real member of the Academy of Sciences."

"Seven minutes?" I was astonished. "How come you didn't show up for three hours?"

"You see, Tolik, when they laid me on that damned table, I began to reconsider: to do or not to do. Well, now I will moan, and you will help me. Okay?"

It was night outside. I lay there and thought, "Here's Ivan Vasilievich. He says, 'Take everything from life you can get.' And he's right. Otherwise, so what? You live, you live, and you get nowhere. Ivan Vasilievich has seen so much. He knows everything, he's been through everything. And me? What have I seen? Or Abram Moiseyevich. What a pest: 'To do, not to do, to do, not to do.' The operation lasted seven minutes, and he thinks about it for a hundred years. Disgusting. You've got to be bold and decisive. Say 'yes' and that's it! Do what you decided. Otherwise it's no good. Otherwise you live your life and see nothing. Like wearing dark glasses. And you only have fifty, sixty years to live. You think that's a lot? Here I am seventeen already, and how the years have flown! You don't even have time to look around. 'Seven times you measure . . .' While you're busy measuring, the time slips by . . . Well, now he's going to groan . . . What a pest!"

Here's to Your Health,

Abram Moiseyevich did not groan. He lay on his back, his yellow hands on the blanket. His sharp nose did not stir, his eyes were wide open. I leaned towards him: he was not breathing.

2

I DIDN'T GET INTO COLLEGE. But somehow I don't feel it was my fault, not in the least.

From the time I was in fifth grade I felt suited to something in the humanities, so I just dropped mathematics, physics, and every kind of chemistry and seriously studied only literature and history. Our literature teacher was Vladimir Valerianovich. A strange man. When I wrote in a composition, according to all the rules, that "the rootless cosmopolitan Jean-Paul Sartre, instigator of a new war, should be brought to trial," Vladimir Valerianovich sighed heavily and said, "Shifrin, I know that you lifted this sentence from yesterday's newspaper. It's good that you know how to use the available sources. . . . But where's your brain? Why do you write things you don't know anything about?" He gave me an A.

Once he brought a book by Zoshchenko to class and read us several stories. We rolled under our desks with laughter, but old Vladimir became completely serious and assigned us a composition on the characteristics of Zoshchenko's language.

Here's to Your Health,

During military training class one day I was reading some Zoshchenko stories, holding the book under my desk. The instructor crept up unnoticed and grabbed the book from my hands.
"What are you reading during class, Shifrin?"
"Just a book."
The instructor took one look at the cover, turned white, and said ominously, "So . . . this is who you're reading. Don't you know the Party pronouncement on this hooligan and enemy?"
"One must study the enemy," I said, looking him straight in the eye.
"What? What did you say?" he said with fright.
"*I* didn't say that—Lenin did."
The class watched our duel with interest.
"I see," said the instructor. "Wait here for me."
He ran into the faculty room.
During the change of classes our director, Alexei Vasilievich, came over to me.
"What are you trying to do? Why are you wrecking our military instructor's lessons? Look out, you're going to get yourself in trouble. . . ."
I didn't argue, because I saw he was reprimanding me just for show. . . .

In our literature textbooks the part about Dostoevsky was printed in small type, and we were happy that we didn't have to read or study him. But old Vladimir devoted two lessons to this Dostoevsky fellow, and afterwards said, "Kids, without considering Tolstoy, Dostoevsky, Platonov, and Babel one can't speak seriously about Russian literature."
Well, I'll admit that Tolstoy is, as Lenin said, "a mirror of the Russian Revolution," but no one even reads the other three. . . .

16

Comrade Shifrin!

In our last year of school we all somehow became very crude. I spoke out at meetings, saying that we should merge the boys' and girls' schools, because having girls in the class might make us behave like gentlemen. But the head teacher told me to cut out this nonsense, because who was I to discuss government decisions, and there were plenty of other people to take care of such things.

"If something is decided, they'll let us know," he said.

We were bored to death during our last year in school, and we amused ourselves as best we could.

Our logic teacher was Asya Grigorievna. Because of her, in my last year I received a B in deportment. She had this fringed shawl, you see. Rafka Raskin, Lenka Kislayev, and I agreed that towards the end of the month, one day during class, we would quietly cut off the fringe. And, fools that we were, we did just that. Always the same story.

I raised my hand and said, "Asya Grigorievna, a question of logic has occurred to me."

She was delighted with my active participation.

"Please, Shifrin, go ahead."

I muttered some nonsense, and Lenka and Rafka yelled from their seats, "Oh, how interesting! A fascinating question. Asya Grigorievna, enlighten us. What Shifrin is asking is just what was bothering us all the time, but we couldn't put it into words. How awfully interesting!"

And we beset poor Asya Grigorievna from all sides. I looked her in the eye as she answered. Lenka distracted her from one side, and Rafka crept up behind her and snipped the fringe off her shawl with a pair of manicure scissors. What idiots! Finally she realized that we were making fun of her, and she kicked us out of class.

We went into the gym on the second floor to toss a

Here's to Your Health,

ball around. The door was locked, and we had to crawl through a hole. (On one side of the gym there were windows and a glass door, all covered by plywood for protection. About six feet above the ground the plywood had come off, and there was a hole just big enough for us to crawl through into the gym.) Once you had crawled through, no one could see from the corridor who was in the gym. This suited us fine.

Rafka and Lenka had already crawled into the gym, and I had only my head and chest inside, legs still sticking out into the corridor, when someone grabbed me by the foot. Struggling to get free, I kicked someone. Suddenly I heard with horror the voice of Alexei Vasilievich, our director.

"So, you want to fight?"

I rolled down into the gym and whispered, "Guys, I kicked old Alexei Vasilievich. If he catches us, he'll throw us out of school for sure."

While the director and the cleaning woman looked for the key to open the gym, we let ourselves out the window, crawled down a drainpipe into the schoolyard, and ran into the classroom through the back door.

During the change of classes Alexei Vasilievich went around to all the senior classes and looked at everyone's feet. I was scared stiff, as I was wearing boots (Papa's combat boots). He said to me, "Come into my office."

I went in. There were six other people there. All wearing boots. (After the war many kids were still wearing their fathers' boots.)

The director came in and said, "Some good-for-nothing just kicked me with his boot. Which one of you did it?"

We all said, "Oh, no! How could that have happened? What a thing to do!"

"Cut it out. If you confess, I'll suspend the culprit from school; if you don't confess, I'll suspend you all.

Comrade Shifrin!

And I don't care if you *are* seniors. What shameful behavior, to strike the director!"

"We were in class," we said.

"From your insolence, I can see that you have completely lost your schoolboy's conscience. But I suspect that Shifrin did it. Am I right, Shifrin?"

I said in mock horror, "What are you saying, Alexei Vasilievich?! What am I, an idiot, to kick the director?"

"Do you hear how he answers? He should be mercilessly thrown out of school."

The other kids began to whine, "Forgive him, Alexei Vasilievich! He won't do it again! Forgive him, please. . . ."

I also whined and we sang like snuffling beggars in front of a church.

"All right, but all the same I'm going to slap a B in deportment on him for the term."

And that's just what he did.

But this is all nonsense, because I nonetheless kept at my studies, intent on winning a medal. My aim was to get a B in algebra, geometry, and trigonometry and an A in all the other subjects. And I would have succeeded if I hadn't been such an ass. Here I must tell you about our physics teacher. Not a bad guy, but such a jerk! He talked in a monotone and without feeling. And for some reason we nicknamed him the "Tatar." Once we had a tutorial in physics before an exam, and when he walked into the classroom I said, "Sergei Vadimich, we can't meet today."

"Why not?" he asked in his indifferent monotone.

"They're deporting Tatars today," I said sympathetically.

"Very well," he replied. "Then I'll leave. But, Shifrin, you can kiss that A in physics good-bye."

He left the room. No one even laughed, and Vovka Mulin said to me, "You idiot."

I got an extra B. And I didn't get a medal.

19

Here's to Your Health,

"So what?" I said to myself. "Millions of children all over the country haven't gotten medals; they'll pass the entrance exam and go to college. Why should I be better than the others?"

I went to enroll in journalism school. I thought I would make a good editor. Long ago I began preparing myself to enter an editorial program. In class, if I came out with some new idea, everyone would gasp with wonder, and the teachers would say, "Look at Shifrin, he's got a head on his shoulders." But it had nothing to do with a head; I simply read college books instead of the boring high school texts. And I had no problems with Russian: the teachers even gave me my classmates' dictations and compositions to correct. I confess I gave B's and A's to my friends, even to Rafka Raskin, who wrote "mowse." I was very sure of myself.

There was stiff competition to get into college—twelve people for each opening. The entrance exam dictation was tricky, and an unprepared candidate could make from two to five mistakes in writing each word. But I knew these idiotic dictations by heart: "Apolinaria Nikitichna, the mischievous bookkeeper, assisted the committee in its thoroughly innocuous endeavors. . . ."

I wrote a perfect dictation. Then the oral exams began. I knew all the questions, and answered them rapid fire. The geography examiner:

"Where is such-and-such . . . ?"

I: "Rat-a-tat!"

Geography examiner: "Correct. C. Next candidate."

History examiner: "Please name for me . . ."

I: "Rat-a-tat!"

History examiner: "Correct. C. Next."

Literature examiner: "Tell us about . . ."

I: "Rat-a-tat!"

Literature examiner: "Correct. C. Next."

Comrade Shifrin!

They all gave me C's! I walked around like a madman. What was going on? In the corridor the historian said to me, "There's nothing you can do about it. That's the way it has to be."

"What do you mean—'that's the way it has to be'?"

But he had already walked away without looking around.

I was beginning to understand. They didn't want me to become an editor! They were purposely giving me C's! And then they said that I didn't do well in the competition.

I grabbed my documents so I could apply to other schools. A lot of good that would do! They wouldn't even talk to me. It was a lost cause. No college this year!

I walked down the stairs sadly, thinking that, in fact, I was miserable. The chairman of the admissions committee walked towards me.

"Why do you look so glum, young man?"

"They didn't accept me to the college. What can I do?"

"Well, it's too early to get upset. Go try a different faculty."

"Which faculty?"

"Oh, let's say, mechanics. You'll be a mechanical engineer. It will suit you very well."

"What do you mean?" I said. "Some engineer I'd make! I never studied any of those subjects in school, I always copied the answers from my classmates. Anyway, I want to be an editor."

"An editor—that's impossible," he said. "But you can still be a mechanical engineer. We haven't filled our quota for the mechanics faculty. Submit your documents there."

"What kind of exams do they have?"

"It's a breeze: algebra, geometry, trigonometry—written and oral—physics, chemistry, and language. That's all. Think about it. Why, I'll even give you five

Here's to Your Health,

whole days to prepare for all of them. Today is the twenty-second of August. If you pass, you'll start classes on September first. Good-bye."

He walked on, and I stood there feverishly trying to figure out what to do. As soon as it dawned on me that all the kids would be going to college while I, wretch that I was, would be hanging around from morning to night with nothing to do, I froze. I wanted to go to college! And when you came right down to it, what difference did it make what I was studying to be? So I'd be a mechanical engineer. It was still a college education, and I wanted to go to college!

I hurried to the admissions office and submitted my application to the mechanics faculty. As I left the office, some timid boys wearing glasses were milling in the hall.

"What exam are you taking?" I asked.

"Physics, for the mechanics faculty," they replied mournfully, their noses buried in fat tomes labeled *Advanced Physics*.

I gazed in dismay at this horrible book and thought that I'd never in my life be able to master it.

"What's the examiner like?"

"Not bad; he's all right."

I singled out the four-eyes who looked the smartest and said, "I'll pass you a note and you hand me the crib sheet, okay?"

"Okay."

I entered the room and selected an examination sheet. Seating myself at a table, I conscientiously copied the contents of the exam on a piece of paper. Then I winked to one of the students who was about to be examined and surreptitiously slipped him the paper. He recited his answers and went out into the corridor, while I waited patiently for my four-eyes. Five minutes later he came in, chose a paper for himself, and, passing my table, threw the crib sheet down in front of me. I

Comrade Shifrin!

studied it, unable to understand a word, copied it all down, and presented myself for examination. (When using a crib sheet, you have to behave in such a way that the instructor is absolutely convinced you know the subject twice as well as he does.) I recited my speech from the crib sheet, emphasizing the points that seemed important. (At these points I would look the instructor in the eye as if to say, "Is that clear?") The third question was a mathematical problem. Four-eyes had written down the solution, but I couldn't make heads or tails of it. I said, "I've gotten an unusually elegant problem, and I think I've devised an amusing solution. Please, look—I think this is a particularly beautiful formula, don't you agree?" The instructor agreed.

"Thatta boy!" Four-eyes congratulated me in the corridor. "You're a whiz!"

"Shifrin—A," announced the instructor, emerging from the examination room.

I was trembling. How could this be? So, all I had to do was to con my way past the exams, and I was an engineering student! Why had I spent five years preparing for admission to the editorial department?

"When's the chemistry exam?"

"Tomorrow," said Four-eyes. "What's your name?"

"Tolya Shifrin. What's yours?"

"Vinogradov, Volodya. Come a little earlier tomorrow. Somehow, it's more fun with you around."

At home that night I got to work on sophomore, junior, and senior chemistry.

I loved our high school chemistry teacher. She was old, stout, and very scatterbrained. Once she had received a decoration for many years' service. We asked her to tell us what it was like there in the Kremlin. To us it was a great mystery; we knew only that Stalin lived there. When we would walk past the Kremlin and see a lighted window, someone invariably would say with love and respect, "Stalin is working." We thought that Stalin never slept: there was always a lighted window in the Kremlin.

And here our chemistry teacher had managed to get inside the Kremlin, which was closed to us, in order to receive her decoration. She told her story:

"We approached the Kremlin. There were many of us. Some man came up and ordered us to enter through the Spassky Gate. We went on. Whenever we'd stop, some very polite young men would come up to us and repeat, 'Keep moving, keep moving, don't fall behind.' And we entered a big hall. It was very bright there. We didn't know where the light was coming from. And then in walked the government. We were all so excited that we wanted to shout 'Hurrah!' And we shouted 'Hurrah,' and they gave us our decorations, a high government award. And then the same young men quickly led us to the exit. Oh, I'll never forget that day. I was so very, very happy."

This is how she performed experiments in the lab:

"Let's pick up this test tube with two fingers of the right hand. Now with the left hand, also with two fingers, let's take up this solution and pour it carefully into the first test tube without stirring it up."

A frightening explosion ensued. Thick, black smoke poured through the chemistry lab, and we were enraptured. Rafka Raskin lay on the floor pretending to be dead. Lenka Kislayev knelt beside him in mourning. I conducted, as the class sang in chorus the old army song, "If a comrade is wounded in battle, his girlfriend will bind up his fresh wounds."

"Just look at you!" The chemistry teacher took offense. "Evidently you're all convinced that the experiment was a failure."

Comrade Shifrin!

I looked at the chemistry textbook and kicked myself for never having studied the subject in which I was to be tested the following day.

The next morning I met Vovka Vinogradov, and we made plans to steal the exam questions. When the instructor entered the room, we were already standing by the table. We watched deferentially as she produced the examination papers and arranged them on the table.

"Excuse me," said Vovka. "Have we come too early?"

"Not at all. I'll just take off my coat, and then you can choose an examination paper."

I helped her with her coat, while Vovka snatched an exam from the table and stuffed it in his pocket.

"We'd like to study a little more," I said, and we went out into the corridor.

We had exam number thirteen—a lucky one.

I memorized the answers to the questions and went in to be tested. At first I stalled a little. Trembling, I began to finger the papers lying on the table.

"Go on, be more confident," said the instructor.

I crossed my legs, crossed my fingers, closed my eyes tight, spit three times over my shoulder, and picked out a set of questions.

"Well?" she prompted.

"Thirteen," I whispered with terror.

"It's nothing to worry about, it happens," she smiled.

I staggered over to the table, sat down, held my head in my hands, and froze. Then I hid the paper I had just chosen in my pocket and took out ours, number thirteen. Everything was in order. I calmed myself and asked permission to answer.

"You see," said the instructor, "it's not so awful."

I breezed through the questions. When she added a question about the properties of iron, I smiled and told her about the fate of the daughter of the great chemist

Mendeleyev, and how she was loved by the famous poets Blok and Bely. She listened with undisguised interest. Vovka and I got A's.

The written math exam went like a dream. I looked at the blackboard speckled with signs and numbers, and I knew that I was an absolute ass. "Oh, well, it looks like I'm not going to get into college this year," I thought. "Such is life. *C'est la vie.*"

There were two variant problems on the blackboard, and Vovka had the one on the left. I was supposed to solve the other one. Vovka, his tongue sticking out in concentration, was writing the last lines of the solution. I picked up my pen and copied everything he had written on his scratch paper. I copied everything—curlicues, x's, scratches, and slips of the pen. I reproduced all the blots and crossed out numbers where Vovka had crossed them out. Then I spit for good luck and handed in my "work."

The next morning we found out that Vovka had gotten a B and I had gotten an A. I said to Vovka, "If you ask me, I'm a regular genius."

He readily agreed with me. I was glad that he didn't bear me a grudge for his B.

The oral math I almost flunked. They had already taken away the textbook and the crib sheet I had hidden under my desk (true, I had said that they weren't mine), and the instructor was looking askance at me. Suddenly some guy came in, exchanged whispers with the examiner, and cheerfully announced, "Gentlemen, you will please address your answers to me."

I rushed up to him with no idea of what to say or where to begin. His eyes were kind and he smelled of beer. He sniffled and tried to keep a straight face.

While he wiped his eyeglasses, I rapidly muttered some tongue-twisting nonsense and then shut up, looking him straight in the eye.

"Is that all?" he asked.

Comrade Shifrin!

"All!" I said firmly.

"And the third question?"

I didn't know the answer to the third question. Suddenly I felt drained. Nothing made any difference anymore. Nothing—not this senseless fuss over the right to go to college, not these stupid tricks—nothing. The whole world seemed loathsome. As if I had just buried my best friend. I thought, "They can go to hell—I'll go to Siberia, to a construction project, or I'll become a librarian somewhere, or an alcoholic."

The instructor was waiting for an answer.

I said quietly to him, "I can't answer the third question."

He raised his eyebrows in surprise and looked me in the eye. He kept on staring at me and suddenly I had the feeling he understood something.

"Hmmm . . ." There was a glint in his eye. "What's your last name?" he asked.

"Shifrin. My name is Shifrin."

"What's wrong with you, Shifrin?" he roared. "You were answering so brilliantly, and now you get stuck on such a simple question. I can't give you an A. I'll give you a B. Aren't you ashamed?"

My eyes filled with tears. "Thank you," I said. "Thank you."

On the twenty-ninth of August they posted the scores. I was second, with twenty-three points out of a possible twenty-five. The passing mark was seventeen.

I strutted, proud as a peacock.

"We engineers," I said, "always solve problems placed before us with courage and boldness." I gave my friends a condescending handshake and clapped them on the shoulder in a fatherly fashion. "I remember, in the old days, you would design something outstanding and everyone would come crawling to you—'Explain, please clarify, dear Comrade Shifrin.' You got tired, you

Here's to Your Health,

know, with one job after another." I was feeling good. I had done well in the competition. I hadn't disgraced my mother. I was going to be an engineer.

The secretary came out and posted the list of those admitted to college.

"Make way for the geniuses and honors students!" I shouted, pushing my way through the crowd towards the list. "Let the members of the Academy of Sciences take a look at their names."

"Shapkin, Shilov, Yasnov—Shapkin, Shilov, Yasnov . . ." I read aloud.

The name Shifrin was not on the list.

"God damn it," I said. "These typists never get anything straight." To omit from the list of candidates one who so brilliantly passed the entrance exams—this was more than just carelessness. There were butterflies in my stomach. I had had a feeling something like this would happen.

"Imagine," I said to the dean, "it's ridiculous. The typists made a mistake and left my name off the list of people accepted to the college."

"No, Comrade Shifrin, the typists had nothing to do with it. It's *we* who decided to reject you, so to speak."

"What do you mean? There's some sort of mix-up here. Look, I got twenty-three points out of a possible twenty-five."

"That's just the point," the dean explained. "You told me, you remember, that you have applied to the humanities faculty. Right? Consequently, you have aptitude for the humanities. We're not certain you will study in our faculty, and we decided to refrain, so to speak, from accepting you into the college."

"Excuse me," I said, "this is a competition system. I took the examinations and scored the required number of points. They have to accept me! I want to go to college!"

"Comrade Shifrin," the dean made a wry face. "I

Comrade Shifrin!

have clearly explained, you see, the essence of the matter, so to speak. You will receive a letter of rejection stating that you did not do well in the competition."

I wanted to lay hold of his fat, ugly face. I wanted to grab him, rip his clothes off. I felt like I was being strangled. Why was this happening to me? Why?

"I know why you won't accept me into college," I whispered, bringing my face close to his. "I know, and I'm not going to let this matter rest. I'm going to Stalin."

He looked at me with eyes full of hate and said calmly, "Please do, Comrade Shifrin. That is your right, so to speak."

I don't remember leaving the college. I was seeing red. Mama, my mama. . . . What would I tell Mama? What had I done to deserve this? What had I done?

I walked along Sadovaya Street. It seemed like a prison yard. March around the circle, around and around the circle! No talking! Hands behind your backs! What a nightmare. What had I done to deserve this? Where should I go? To Stalin? But he had so much work, what did he need with some kid who wasn't accepted to college? Did I dare tear Stalin away from his work?! Oh, if he only knew what kind of scoundrels he had under him, he would let them have it! But they were vermin. They took advantage of the fact that Stalin was busy, and they played dirty tricks, they played dirty tricks. What was I going to do?

I decided to go to the Ministry of Higher Education. I'd walk up to the minister and say to him, "Comrade Minister. I want to go to college!" He'd say to me, "Yes, Comrade Shifrin, they treated you very unfairly. The Soviet state still has many enemies. I thank you for your help in denouncing them." Then he'd pick up the phone and call Comrade Stalin. "Iosif Vissarionovich," he'd say. "Comrade Shifrin here is telling us about some interesting goings-on in our colleges. What are your instructions, Comrade Stalin?" And Stalin would say, "Punish those who made trouble for Comrade Shifrin, and admit him to college, Comrade Minister." My God, what was I saying? What would I do? What would I do? . . . Oh, yes, the Ministry . . .

There was a long line at the entrance to the Ministry. Boys and girls alike were standing there, with parents and without, blondes and brunettes, with and without glasses, fat and skinny, well-dressed and poorly dressed. And not one of them had gotten into college.

"How many points did you get?" I asked one person, a second, and a third. . . .

"Twenty-nine out of thirty . . . Moscow Aviation Institute."

"Twenty-four out of twenty-nine. Moscow Technical College."

"Gold medal. Moscow State University."

They stood in a silent line, clutching textbooks and looking straight ahead with unseeing eyes. I also took my place at the end of this strange line and became one of them, and all of us looked like brothers and sisters crowded around the entrance to the big building.

"Why were you rejected?"

"I don't know. . . ."

"It's all nonsense," said a fat fellow in a white scarf. "My dad will call the right person, and everything will be o.k.!"

"That's fine for you," said a little guy with glasses. "You have someone to call. . . ."

"So call your own connection," the fat one got excited. "If I had your marks, I know what I'd do! . . . Where does your father work?"

"I don't have a father," said the little guy with the glasses.

"What, was he killed during the war?"

"No. . . . He's in Siberia . . . working. . . ."

Comrade Shifrin!
A girl in a pink blouse said nervously, "My father is missing in action. But Mama says that he's alive. . . . I have a medal. . . ."
"Strange. . . ."
A black-haired youth said, without lifting his eyes from his book, "There's nothing strange about it. My father told me a thousand times, 'Be an engineer.' But I wanted to be a critic. It wasn't meant to be, I guess."
"Why were you rejected, Shifrin?"
"I don't know," I said, walking away from the crowd.
After two weeks had passed I got to see some sort of big-shot in the Ministry. He was eating an apple, a crisp, noisy apple.
"What's on your mind, make it quick," he said, crunching on his apple with pleasure.
I told my story. He looked at that apple, and, choosing the most appetizing places, sank his teeth into it and smacked his lips. When I had finished, he swallowed the seeds and said, "They were right. I'd rather take some *Choochmek* from Central Asia than you."
"Why?"
"After graduation a *Choochmek* will work, at least, but *you*. . . ."
"My God," I moaned, "I'll work, too. Accept me. Look, I passed all the tests. I've earned it."
"No, it's impossible. That's all!"
I walked out of his office and started to cry. I understood that nothing could be done to help me. And the tears didn't make me feel any better.
But at that moment opportunity was walking down the corridor, dressed in a shabby wool suit and unpolished shoes, a bald spot on his head.
"Why are you crying, son?"
"They didn't accept me to college," I said through my tears.
"What's your name, son?"
"Shifrin."

Here's to Your Health,

The man sighed. "So that's it. Come into my office." On his door was written: Chief Personal Inspector for the Minister.

He took my documents and told me to call in two weeks.

For two weeks I wandered aimlessly about the streets. All my friends were in college, and here I was wandering about the streets. I went a little crazy. I thought constantly about the man in the wool suit. At last I called him.

"You're going to study in the correspondence college. Not in the mechanics faculty, but in the technological faculty. Is that all right?"

My God—mechanics, technology, geography, cubology—what difference did it make! I was going to college! To college! To college! To college!

"Thank you," I said, "thank you."

The boys and girls were still standing at the entrance to the Ministry, looking straight ahead with unseeing eyes. . . .

3

THERE WERE FIVE of us students in the correspondence school. We had all met approximately the same fate, and we sank our teeth into our studies as if we had come from a land of famine. We polished off our subjects the way heavy-weight boxers polish off novices. By the end of the first semester, we had already passed all the first year exams. Now we could take a look around us.

What lay ahead? The army. It knocked at my door in the form of an induction notice ordering me to appear for service. Correspondence students were not allowed the exemption given to those who had matriculated. Correspondence students had to serve. I appeared at the induction center.

"Comrade Shifrin," the major said to me. "You will serve in the tank corps. How do you like that?"

"Not much, Comrade Major."

"Why not?"

"Just an unaccountable feeling, Comrade Major."

"Come, come, don't stall, Shifrin. How about the navy?"

"I want to go to college, Comrade Major."

"College? Do you know what, we'll send you to college. Special recruitment. Naval academy."

"Is that higher education?"

"Advanced engineering."

I imagined myself in bell-bottomed trousers, striped shirt, sailor hat. Girls walking toward me. Who's this dashing sailor? Look, it's Tolya Shifrin. What a man he's become! Is it hard duty, Tolya? Well, how can I tell you? It's hardest of all when the wind reaches gale force. You stand on the bridge, chilled to the marrow, but you grip the helm tightly. Like this, you hold on. You think I'm kidding? This is not your puny landlubber. It's no joke. . . . As the song goes, "The girls eye us with interest, we're sailors from Odessa."

"Well, how about it, Shifrin? I'm sending you for a physical."

"Yes, sir, Comrade Major!"

"Well now, that's more like it."

About fifty men from Moscow were chosen for the naval academy. They sent us all for physicals. The doctors rejected forty-eight as unfit. They passed two, me and one other, a judo expert. I was thin as a rail; you could see me only in profile. The doctor pinched my skinny muscles and said, "The navy will put some meat on you."

The major said, "You're a lucky fellow, Shifrin, to have passed the physical! That's all for now. The head of the personnel department of the naval academy is coming soon—a full captain. You will speak with him. Good-bye and good luck!"

The captain arrived three weeks later. He interviewed us at the induction center. I already felt like a regular sailor. When he called me, I clicked my heels, came to attention, and reported, "Shifrin, Anatoli, at your command!"

The captain took a liking to me from behind the table and growled in a fatherly voice, "You'll be a dashing officer. Are you ready, Comrade Shifrin?"

"Yes, sir, Comrade Captain!"

Comrade Shifrin!

"Very well. Major, bring me Comrade Shifrin's file."
The major ran out to get my file, and in the meantime the captain chatted with me about life. Were my parents alive, how did I do in school, how about discipline? The major brought in the folder. The captain opened it, glanced at the application, and suddenly his jaw dropped and his eyes widened like saucers. He looked at the major and said to him, "What's wrong with you, Major? Have you lost your mind?"

"What's the matter?"

"What's the matter!? Is this some sort of joke? . . ." He caught sight of me. "You—march into the corridor, we'll call you."

From behind the plywood door I eavesdropped on their conversation.

Captain: "What are you trying to put over on me, Major? Don't you know the rules?"

Major: "I'm sorry, Comrade Captain, it was an oversight. He really doesn't look like one."

Captain: "Look like one!? You'd better look here, it's all written down. Are you blind?"

Major: "I'm sorry, these things happen. What should we do with him now?"

Captain: "What indeed! Send him to the army, the infantry."

Major: "I'll send him to tank school. Shifrin! Come in here."

I went in, an innocent smile stretching from ear to ear. Good soldier Schweik.

"What are you grinning about, Shifrin?" the major asked sternly. "And why are you standing there like that? Look, unfortunately there is no more room in the naval academy. We're sending you to tank school."

"That's impossible, Major," I said, continuing to smile.

"What do you mean—'no'!?" The major exploded. "We'll send you—and you'll go!"

35

"That's impossible, Major," I obstinately repeated.
The major's shouts sounded like breakers far out on the ocean: "Call-up papers... appear with your belongings... don't leave town...."

I felt awful. A lump in my throat prevented me from speaking. The smile stayed glued to my face. I couldn't get rid of it.

Outside it was spring. Muddy streams of water ran down the sidewalks, carefully avoiding the blocks of gray snow which lay in their path. The air smelled of sparrows. Dirty icicles smashed to pieces in the drain pipes. My heart was cold. I didn't have a heart at all.

I don't know myself how I got to the college. Carefree students ran past me. What did they have to worry about, they didn't have to go to tank school. The world's shortest joke: Shifrin of the tank corps.

The admissions office was already open. A girl sat in the room, the same girl to whom I had submitted my application the previous year.

"Hi!" I said. "Do you still need students?"

"We do," she said.

"I'm here for the second-year course. I'm from the correspondence division."

"Okay, we have a large drop-out rate for the second-year course. Let's see your application."

"What do you mean?" I asked. "That can't be."

"Why not?" she replied. "What's the matter with you? Let's see your application, show me your grades for the first year."

Two minutes later she emerged from the director's office. Across the report was written in red pencil: "Accepted for the second-year course."

I passed out. That is, I vanished somewhere. When I opened my eyes, the frightened girl stood over me holding a glass of water.

Comrade Shifrin!

"What's wrong with you?" she said, "are you all right?"

"A certificate," I whispered. "Proof, right here, that I'm a student. A full-time day student. In the second-year course."

I clutched the certificate in my right hand, and my right hand in my left for safekeeping. I strode purposefully to the induction office. Outside it was spring. Clean, sparkling streams of water ran down the sidewalks, carrying away the remains of the dirty snow. It smelled sunny. Icicles jingled merrily in the drainpipes, singing spring marches. In my heart it was spring. My heart was beating like the clock of the Spassky Tower.

"Well, Shifrin," the major greeted me. "Be here tomorrow with your belongings. And don't be late!"

"That's impossible, Major," I said, handing him my cherished certificate. In walked the captain. He snatched the paper, ran his eyes over it, and said admiringly, "They sure know how to take care of themselves!"

Then he slapped his thigh and repeated, "They sure know how to take care of themselves!"

As I left the room, my back was struck by still another malicious yet enthusiastic, "They sure know how to take care of themselves!"

4

IT WAS A TERRIFYING DAY.
I was walking along the street with my head pulled down between my shoulders, avoiding the faces of passersby. They were broadcasting something shocking over the radio. As usual, I stopped at my corner to buy a newspaper from old Aunt Fanya.
"*Pravda*, please, Aunt Fanya."
"What a terrible thing, Tolya," she said, "what a terrible thing! Why did they do it? What more did they need?"
"What did they do, Aunt Fanya?"
"Oh, they should only leave us alone! Anything can happen now. What trouble they've brought down on our heads!" She swayed from side to side in her kiosk like an upside-down pendulum.
When I got to the college, it was buzzing with the news.
"Tolya, there's a meeting today. We're going to have a discussion," shouted the Komsomol organizer as he ran by.
Everyone in our group was quiet.
"Hi!" I said. "Varya, let me look at the summary."
She jumped away from me as if she had been stung.

Comrade Shifrin!

"Don't touch me!" she shouted. "I hate you! I hate all of you! Don't come near me, you hear! I'm ready to kill you!"

"Idiot," I said, and walked out of the auditorium. Everyone heard what she had shouted at me, and no one stirred.

The whole college was gathered in the assembly hall.

"Vigilance!" the speakers repeated. "Only vigilance!"

It was a terrifying day. That day they had arrested the doctors . . . for planning to murder our leaders, perhaps even Stalin himself.

They took Professor Dunayevsky, too. My God, Professor Dunayevsky. . . .

His death was unthinkable. He couldn't die. People die. But not Him. What will we do without Him? What will Russia do without Him? If He dies, Russia will perish. . . .

5

OUR COLLEGE CLASS was sent to a collective farm to dig potatoes. We complained, we balked, but the secretary of the Komsomol committee said that if we didn't go, we'd have only ourselves to blame for the consequences. In the second place, he said, it was our duty to help the kolkhozniks, and, thirdly, in such weather only idiots would refuse to go the country to breathe some fresh air. "Hay, milk—what more could you ask for?" said the secretary. We went.

The village was called Ozera. To get there, you ride three hours from Moscow on the electric suburban train, then you go by truck down a winding, dusty road about twenty-five miles off the rail line. All around are fields of yellowing grain, intersected by utility poles strung with sagging wires. And then through a forest, green and fragrant. . . . The forest ends suddenly, and a village is spread out before you. Ozera! There's a single long street with chickens wandering lazily about. Houses line either side, each with three windows facing the street. From one of these houses hangs a faded, gray flag, announcing the village soviet.

Hoarse from the dust and from singing, we jumped

Comrade Shifrin!

out of the truck and threw our knapsacks into a pile. We had arrived!

The unshaven chairman walked out on the porch of the soviet building and scratched his ear. A crumpled winter cap sat on the back of his head.

"So, you've arrived, kids?"

"Here we are!"

"Who's in charge?"

"Galka Amurova."

"Well, Galka-Palka, let's find quarters for your regiment. Tomorrow we go into the fields. Take the boys to Prokhor's, there's lots of room there. And have the girls go to Ustinia's—she's expecting them."

The boys—that meant me. I was to go to Prokhor's.

"Lookee here," laughed the chairman. "It's the same in Moscow as in the village. Only women. What's happened to the boys?"

"Our college is like that," Galka tried making excuses. "Boys don't like to go there."

"Ah," nodded the chairman, "so that's it. It's the same story here. . . . Now, off you go."

I took my little suitcase and followed a barefoot boy, who wasn't the least bit interested in me.

"What's your name?"

"Kolka."

"Why don't you say something, Kolka?"

"What do you want me to say?" he lisped. "You guys from Moscow, you're all the same. 'What's your name? How old are you? Where's your mama? Why doesn't your daddy work on the kolkhoz?' What do you think I am? Why do you ask so many questions? You guys from Moscow are all the same. . . . Every year, it never fails, you come here. . . ."

"You're a smart one, Kolka. . . ."

"This here's Prokhor's house. So long!"

" 'Bye, Kolka."

41

Here's to Your Health,

I knocked at the low door of a hut standing at the very end of the street.

"T'ain't locked," answered a high, hoarse voice.

"I'm from Moscow. I came to dig potatoes. ..."

"Come on in, what you waiting for?"

"Hello, I ..."

"I already see. Well—so you were sent by Kuzya from the soviet, were you?"

"Uh-huh."

"You'll sleep over there, it's softer. I bet your bones are educated, need a soft bed."

"Oh no. I'm a hiker. I'll do it the Spartan way, so to speak."

"Hmm," he nodded, "hear that a lot on the radio—Spartacus this, Spartacus that. ... So you're a Spartacus?"

Prokhor sat down at the table and stared at me with squinting, dark eyes. On the table lay a crumpled pack of cigarettes. Prokhor looked about sixty. His broad-lipped, beardless face was attractive; an ironic smile played about the corners of his mouth as he asked that mocking question about Spartacus.

"No, I'm not a Spartacus. I'm Tolya."

"Well, well, glad to meet you! Want something to eat?"

"No, thanks, we had a snack."

"Well, then sit yourself down, we'll listen to the radio."

I lay down on the bench and covered myself with my coat, while Prokhor worked some magic at the old "box" ("loudspeaker," as it was called before the war). He settled down to listen.

It was warm and stuffy in the hut, and I couldn't keep my eyes open. As I dozed off I heard the measured voice of the announcer interspersed with Prokhor's mumbled comments.

Comrade Shifrin!

"The kolkhozes of the Kharkov region fulfilled their grain delivery plan. The granaries of our country are filled with more than . . . tons. . . . The farmers have made us all a wonderful present. . . ."

"Farmers," mumbled Prokhor, "where are they, these farmers? Huh. . . ."

"In the Warsaw competition first prize was won by the young Soviet violinist . . ."

"Whaddya know," grumbled Prokhor, "you sawed away, sawed away, got first prize. Send him to a kolkhoz, that'd be some first prize!"

"Awake, Octobrists and Pioneers, the Revolution's call is clear!" A bugle seemed to be blaring into my ear. I started and looked around.

"Why are you jumping about?" Prokhor muttered from somewhere behind the stove. "Never heard a rooster?"

"No, I never have," I said, yawning. I couldn't go back to sleep. My back was all stiff. I grunted and rolled onto my other side.

"When do you have to be at work, Uncle?"

"I've already worked my share. With interest."

"How's that? You're a member of the kolkhoz, aren't you?"

"So what? Nowadays everyone belongs. But I do other things. Fix a stove, or, say, a roof needs patching —they call me."

"Ah. . . . So that means you don't work on the land?"

He was silent.

"Have you been in Ozera long, Uncle?"

"I'm living here for the second time."

"What do you mean, 'the second time?' "

"Well, might as well tell you about it. . . . You've still got a lot to learn."

"Tell me, I can't sleep anyway. . . ."

Here's to Your Health,

I couldn't see Prokhor in the dark. I looked out a little window which framed a bit of sky with clouds floating through it. I listened.

"I was born right here in this place, in Ozera. And my father lived his life here. He was married in Ozera. We were two kids. Me and my brother Egor. This place was all rye. You know, we worked rye. Our papa was a hard worker. A real peasant, that is. Well, then along comes the Revolution. We'll give you land, they say. Well, the peasants, sure, were all for that! They cut up the land, started to farm.... My papa always said to me, 'Proshka, the land is like a mama; she warms you and feeds you and gives you the breast. If you don't love the land—get yourself to the city, because she won't be good to you or anyone else.' And me and Egor, we took to farming.... We sowed, and plowed, and harvested. ... You know, like everybody. The farmland here is good. We didn't starve. And then comes the order: collectivize. The muzhiks have a meeting. Papa goes, too. They decide to get together, try it out. If it's worse than before, we'll break it up. Let's do what the government wants before they do it for us. So . . . our land was no black soil, we weren't no kulaks. But the farmers were making a good living; one had a horse; another, a cow or two. . . . If someone needed help, the neighbors would pitch in. Today, you help me—tomorrow, I help you. To speak in their way, all of us were middle peasants.

"And then from Moscow a commission comes. I'll never forget it. The chief—a monster! They set up down in the village soviet, call muzhiks up one by one. They call up papa. The chief tells him, 'Give us the buried seed that you didn't turn over!' Papa says, 'We gave it all. Just kept a little for the animals for winter, and for our own food. The harvest was bad, too much sun.' The chief says, 'Turn over that grain and call the

Comrade Shifrin!

next man. Tomorrow morning we're taking it all away.'

"Papa says, 'Comrade, you're a good man—how can I give it to you? What'll I eat, and my kids, and my animals—what'll they eat? I don't have any extra, I need it to live.' The chief bangs on the table. 'You bastard,' he yells, 'you damned kulak, you'll get fat on grain, and the working class will starve on account of you! Turn over the grain, I say, and go get the next man. Do you think,' he says, 'we came here to have a discussion with you? All of you fat little kulaks,' he says, 'are trying to pull the same trick! The Soviet government is your sworn enemy! To the triumphal end!'

"My father turned black with rage and said, 'I won't turn it over.' And he walked out. They came at night. When they started to tear up the floor, Egorka couldn't take it anymore. He grabbed a bench and threw it at the chief. They killed Egorka right there.... Shot and killed him. And in the morning the soldiers came, put us in carts. They took practically everyone. From all over Russia. In cattle cars. Maybe you heard the saying, 'Eight horses—forty men?' Well, they loaded a hundred of us in one car. Papa died on the way. He didn't make it to the taiga. And when he was dying, he says to me, 'They're killing the peasants. Beating them to death. Who's going to work the land?'

"They shipped us to the snows, unloaded us. We started living in earthen huts. Spent the winter in 'em. And many died off.... But man is such a creature, he can hang on almost anywhere. So we did. We lived through it, built little huts. Lived by hunting. Like real Siberians! I don't know how we did it. And then we were put to work. Some went into timber, some went into fishing, others went into the mines. I became a miner. From working on the earth to crawling beneath it.... You ever see a mine? No? God keep you from it. ... It's cruel work. A man turns animal in the mines. He gets meaner and meaner 'til he ain't a man at all.

He ain't afraid of God or the devil. . . . And so he lives from day to day, night to night.

"You come home from work to the settlement, and all around the earth lies untouched, fat, black. . . . You want to take a plow to her, to mother earth. But you can't. After the mines you got no hands, no legs. . . . You just feel dead. After a while, I didn't think about it no more. . . . Sort of lost the habit. . . .

"Then along comes the war. A law comes out: 'The son don't have to answer for his father.' They round us up, take us to fight on the Moscow front. I was wounded. . . . Hey, you, sleeping? No?"

"I'm not sleeping, Uncle Prokhor, I'm listening."

"So. . . . In the end, I come back to Ozera. Nobody left, deserted. . . . No men, only women with little kids sitting around the huts. The land dry, untouched. . . . The kolkhozes overgrown. . . . They'd send chairmen from the city. They'd beat their heads against the wall for a while and run away. Or start to drinking. They would fire them and others would come. And the land was hateful to me. I couldn't stand looking at her. I'd go into a field, and I'd see Egorka and Papa standing before me. An evil spell, that's what it was. . . .

"Then they sent Kuzya to be the chairman. He says to me, 'Prokhor, help society, go into the fields. . . . There is no one who understands the earth,' he says, 'no one's left, you're the only one. Teach the women how to work the land.' "

"Did you do it, Uncle Prokhor?"

"No, I couldn't. I lost the habit. . . . The earth loves a master. For me, she's gone—she turned into a stepmother."

"If they cut you a piece of land, will you go to work?"

Prokhor let himself down from the stove and looked at me with mean, distant eyes.

"No, I won't take it. . . . They're tricking us anyway."

"They're not tricking you, Uncle Prokhor."

Comrade Shifrin!

"No, I wouldn't take it anyway. I'm no peasant anymore. . . ."

We dug the potatoes. They were very pleased with us at the college.

6

I GOT A JOB.

Our printing-plant was big and new, and we printed books and pamphlets for children. The first time I went to see the director, Lev Yakovlevich, he seemed a quiet, small, plain man. He spoke gutturally and never looked you in the eye when he talked to you.

I said, "Good day. I've been assigned to work here."

"So I heard. Sit down, young man, and we'll think up a job for you."

He pressed a button and the secretary Galya came in.

"Call, uh, in here . . . Oh, you know who."

Some technical engineers came in—my future bosses and colleagues.

Lev Yakovlevich pointed at me and said, "This boy's been assigned to us after college. He has an engineer's diploma. Where should we put him?"

The head engineer, a woman, said, "Let him be a controller in the finishing shop."

So I became a controller.

In the mornings I got to work like this: I would wake up when the alarm went off. That was revolting, because the sweetest thing in the world is to sleep a little after the alarm rings. I would jump up and rush into the

Comrade Shifrin!

kitchen. Fix an omelette, easiest thing. An omelette with sausage. Polish sausage. Standing up, I would eat the omelette right from the frying pan and run to catch the bus.

Work began promptly at eight. If I arrived at 8:03, the attendance monitor would report me, and I would be punished for absenteeism and loafing. The idea was to be in your place before eight. I would rush along the street panting in order to punch in on time. I would fly into the printing-plant courtyard—safe! Then, serenely, falling asleep as I walked, I would meander slowly into the office, sit down at my desk, and doze. These drowsy moments were wonderful; I would get lost in reverie, dreaming some wondrous unfinished dream. This time was mine. Finally, I would shake off my torpor and remember that I was a controller. I had to go around to all the shops, see what was doing on the machines, and gather the work orders from the foremen, along with their reports of the previous day's output. Then, I would calculate the production plan, draw up a summary, and give the shops their assignments for that day and the next.

Of course, I couldn't grasp the whole production process right away. I would always forget something. For this reason I invariably appeared ludicrous and stupid at the daily meetings with the director. He treated me indulgently, but always made fun of me.

"Stand up," he said to me at one meeting. "Tell us, what are we sewing on the bookbinding machines?"

I didn't remember, because I hadn't been able to get to all the shops.

"The bookbinders are now working on, uh . . . You know, uh, what's his name . . . ," I stammered.

"Look at him," said the director. "Look at this blockhead with the diploma. He doesn't know what the bookbinders are doing. And what *do* you know, by the way?"

I couldn't say a thing because he was right. In college they taught us everything under the sun except how to get along on a job. I kept silent, looked guiltily at my sympathetic colleagues, and smiled sheepishly.

After work I walked home, thinking about the fact that I was a real clod. But then, what can you do? Somebody's got to be a clod. . . .

One day Lev Yakovlevich called me into his office and said, "Your mind is on everything but your work. We'll never make a controller of you. But maybe you'd be a fantastic *quality* controller."

"Maybe," I said gloomily.

"I'm going to assign you to work with the senior foreman of the quality control section. It will be your job to go around to the shops sniffing out defective goods. If you find shoddy work in my plant—which, of course, is highly unlikely—then you will take steps immediately. We must turn out the highest quality work! Let's say 'no!' to defective products! Soviet children must have only the best books! We must. . . ."

"Okay," I said. "I won't let your defective goods out of here."

So I became a quality controller. Every morning I made the rounds of the shops and checked to see that everything was in good shape.

The shops were pushing hard to meet the production quotas. We were supposed to turn out 80,000 books each day. Any less and they took it out of our hides.

Klavdia Anisimova, the fat, lively boss of the book-stitching shop, always met me at the door.

"For heaven's sake, look who has come to see us," she would say caressingly, shielding piles of defective books with her body. For heaven's sake, Tolenka, we're so glad to see you, so glad . . ."

I felt like a policeman who has just apprehended a

Comrade Shifrin!

truck driver transporting stolen state goods. I was only doing my job.

"Greetings, Madame," I said. "What about these defective books?"

"What defective books?" Klavdia Anisimovna was plainly frightened. "What on earth are you talking about, Tolya dear?"

But I was already walking around the shop, vigilantly examining pamphlets and books waiting to be shipped to stores. The girls in the shop smiled at me and said, "Hello, Anatoli Alexandrovich, why don't you ever come dancing with us?"

"Hello," I muttered sullenly, looking over the output. There was a lot of defective merchandise. But these were "tolerable defects"—the poor quality stuff we see everyday on our store counters not even suspecting it's defective merchandise.

And then my gaze fell on a pile of pamphlets on which was printed *tykov-Shchedr.*

"Klavdia Anisimovna!" I intoned. "Do come over here, my little dove. What could this *tykov-Shchedr* mean?"

"For heaven's sake," said Klavdia Anisimovna, "look at that! What a wonder! That means the book is called *Saltykov-Shchedrin.*"

"Where do you see any *Saltykov-Shchedrin?*" I roared. "This says *tykov-Shchedr,* and the rest has been cut off by the machine; you have some drunken cutter, or the devil knows who, working there. I forbid you to turn this book over to the dispatch office. *Verstehen Sie?*"

"Oh, come on, Tolya," she said seriously. "What do you want to do, ruin my production plan? Deprive the foremen of their bonuses? You'd do better to take a look at what goes on in the binding shop. Talk about defective work! You haven't seen anything yet!"

"Madame," I said in an unbending voice, "I get paid so that you'll produce the highest quality books. Let's say 'no!' to defective goods! Soviet children must have only the best books! We must . . ."

At this point the door flew open and in walked Lev Yakovlevich, surrounded by a glittering retinue. At his right walked the chief engineer; she cast menacing glances everywhere to see if everything was under control. At his left walked the head of the production division, a good-looking woman who had the right to tell the truth to the director's face.

"Lev Yakovlevich," she was saying, "you are wrong! That employee must be punished much more severely!"

A little behind them marched the mechanic Sidorov. He was already a little bit under the influence, and his objectives were, first of all, not to trip and fall, and second, to repair any broken machines. Behind him, at a respectful distance, followed the controllers, foremen, and union organizers. Klara Abramovna, the boss of the quality control department, brought up the rear.

Klavdia Anisimovna flung herself at the director and began to whisper something in his ear, fixing her gaze on me. Her eyes were rolling like bicycle wheels.

"Where?" Lev Yakovlevich asked softly. I didn't like it when he spoke softly. It meant that someone was going to get it.

Ignoring me, he walked up to the shelf of defective *tykov-Shedr*'s.

"Well, what is this?" he asked, looking me in the eye. "What have you found here, Mr. Sherlock Holmes?"

"This is defective work," I said firmly.

"Where is defective work?"

"Right here."

"Uh-huh. And *these* aren't defective?" He poked at a stack of books produced for export.

"No, those are not defective."

Comrade Shifrin!

"How naive can you be?" said the director. "Can't you tell with your young eyes what's defective and what's not? These here are defective goods—reject them," he nodded towards the books intended for export, "and these"—a nod to the ill-fated *tykov-Shchedr*'s —"let them pass. Do you understand me, young man?"
"No," I said. "I don't understand you. It's just the opposite. We must say . . ."
"I'll fire you, you hooligan," the director said calmly. "That will teach you to contradict me. Who's the director, you or me?"
The retinue looked at me sadly and disapprovingly.
"You. You're the director."
"Snotty kid!" shouted Lev Yakovlevich. "Klara Abramovna, fire him right away. I tell him where there is defective work, I teach him, and instead of being grateful, he argues with the director. How do you like that, Klara Abramovna?"
Klara Abramovna walked up to me and whispered, "Don't be an idiot. Do as he says."
But I was all fired up. I declaimed fiercely, "I am a QC, which, in plain language, means quality controller. *That* means I must stand to the death and not allow our plant to be disgraced. I *cannot* allow this defective work. I *will* not allow it!"

The defective *tykov-Shchedr*'s ended up at the central book warehouse. Two days later the telephone rang and a delicious, insolent baritone voice said, "So, what the devil are you sending out, sweetheart? A little defective merchandise? Well, we'll just write up a little report on you. We'll send you a little fine. Your QC must be sitting around twiddling his thumbs."
"Go to hell," I thought maliciously, hanging up on him. I had warned them. I knew this would happen. Klavdia Anisimovna had included these defective *tykov-Shchedr*'s in her production plan, and now there

53

would be an official complaint. . . . Let the director get himself out of this. What's it to me? Spitefully, I wrote a report that ended with the words ". . . about which I duly warned them."

"Shifrin, the director wants to see you," the secretary Galya commanded, on her way to the cafeteria.

As I crossed the threshhold, the director exploded.

"Who is this I see before me! Youth, so to speak, our future! Well, and how's your work going? Is your office drafty? Is everything comfortable?"

"It's uncomfortable," I said. "We'll have more grief over this pamphlet."

"How's that?" he said with surprise. "Why on earth did you pass those defective books?"

I choked with indignation.

"Isn't that a shame?" said the director. "Any second now he's going to explode. Look how he's pouting. An engineer yet! Don't pout—correct your mistakes. Go to the warehouse and arrange it so that they return those books to us without a fuss. Tell them we'll take care of everything. And no more of those ridiculous reports. Writing reports—it's become the latest thing. . . ."

"They're going to write one anyway," I said.

"They're only people, kid, and people are always people."

"Of course, people are always people. And animals are always animals, houses always houses, books always books, and children always children. I'm not disputing that."

"Don't be an idiot. You know very well what I mean. Take the six-volume limited subscription edition of Mayne Reid and go to the warehouse. Pick up the defective Saltykov-Shchedrins and bring them back to the plant."

"And what should I do with Mayne Reid?"

The director pressed a button, and the secretary Galya came in.

Comrade Shifrin!

"Who else is waiting to see me?" the director asked.

I left, grabbed a car, and drove to the warehouse, holding a neat bundle of Mayne Reids on my lap. The owner of the delicious baritone turned out to be a real con artist, a master at his craft. Right away, he asked, "Well, sweetheart, what have you brought me?"

"Mayne Reid," I said without beating around the bush. "I'll give you Mayne Reid, you give me Saltykov-Shchedrin, and no reports."

"I am a law-abiding man." The baritone was offended.

Having completed this Soviet business transaction, we exchanged bows and I returned to home port, satisfied with my work.

"Good boy," said the director. "But all the same, I'm going to take away your bonus for letting defective goods leave the factory."

7

I FINISHED WORK at six o'clock—at least, I was supposed to finish at six. But somehow it never turned out that way. There was always some problem or other in the shop that demanded my attention. I stayed late and swore that tomorrow, God damn it, I'd leave on time. How long could this go on? I was a healthy young man; I should have been thinking about girlfriends, going out, having a good time with my friends. And here I sat like a fool, long after quitting time, forced to nag a little more, tie up loose ends, follow things through, organize a little more. . . . At last, I would walk out the factory door and make my way to the trolleybus. I stopped in book stores along the way, bought books, flirted with the salesgirls. I was very lonely. Then I rode home.

I had been noticing her on the bus for a long time. I got on my bus to go to work at the same time every day. And she was always sitting in the corner of the last seat. When I got in she would lower her eyes to her book. Then she would get out, and I would ride on and watch through the window as she ran to the subway. When I was late for my bus and someone else sat in her seat, it made me feel out of sorts. Once she tore herself away from her book and stared at me. On that occasion, as

Comrade Shifrin!

always, I looked her over and mentally conversed with her. Her eyes were light blue and surprised. We kept looking at one another, and she missed her stop. She gasped, jumped off the bus, and ran to the subway. Astonished, I rode on to work thinking how strange I felt. . . .

There was a burst of activity in our shop. All month we had been producing cheap books, and now we were trying to get ourselves out of the hole. We fulfilled the plan one hundred and fifty percent—but still there was no money. We asked the publishing house for more lucrative work, but the publishing house refused. Our production plan was in danger. We had already decided to give it up as a lost cause (what else could we do?), when the director summoned me and said, "Why do I always have to do your thinking for you? If we don't fulfill our plan, you'll be left without a bonus."

"You yourself know, Lev Yakovlevich . . ."

"I know everything," he said sternly. "I always know everything. You're going to print fish."

"What do you mean—fish?"

"There's an order from some strange publishing house. We have to print in color a hundred fish of all kinds. It's lucrative work. It will boost your statistics. Go and get the type form"

"You're our savior," I intoned. "God will reward you. . . ."

"God doesn't exist," said the director. "If he did, I wouldn't have to put up with you. . . ."

I hurried off to print the fish.

The foremen and I agreed to squeeze as much as possible from those fish.

"And also what is impossible," said Foreman Belov.

So we netted our fish. It was like the big catch of the fishing season. Fish stared at us from all corners of the shop—red fish and blue fish, purple and yellow, gaunt and fatty, head on and in profile. We rubbed our hands

Here's to Your Health,

and wrote the fish into our production plan as a money catch. And at this point I went too far. I decided to make an addition to our plan. I thought that nobody would notice if I falsely reported running off an extra batch of fish. Then we would be able to work calmly during the next month, without panicking to fulfill our production quota. We'd set aside the figures on our surplus output, and next month we would quietly turn in the necessary money to the plan.

We finished the month in great shape and received a citation for exceeding the production quota. We were already getting set to rest peacefully on our laurels—"take a breather," as Foreman Belov put it—when suddenly we were caught by the cost-controller—Nikolai Semyonovich, the old rat. He knew the printing business inside out, and of course he discovered our phoney "extra run". Nikolai Semyonovich raised hell.

"This is intolerable!" he screamed. "What have we come to? Our young people are crooks! Who did he think he would fool? Me? I'm an old-timer in this business, and he pretends innocence with those baby-blue eyes of his! And when the inspector comes, who's going to jail? Nikolai Semyonovich? Not on your life! I wasn't in jail even in thirty-seven, and I'm not about to go now. What a wise-guy!"

"Calm down, Nikolai Semyonovich," I said. "It was an error. We weren't paying attention, and we made a mistake. We'll correct it. What do you think I'm doing, taking something for myself? The government . . ."

"Shifrin, the director wants to see you," said the secretary Galya, on her way to the cafeteria.

The director was, in the poet's words, silent as a Ukrainian night. He looked out the window and drummed his fingers against the glass.

The supervisors filed in one by one. When everyone was gathered, the director said, "Well, I know how to deal with this cheat, this liar, this parasite—he's going

Comrade Shifrin!

straight to jail. But where were you during all this? Some assistants I've got! Any schoolboy can make fools of them if he has a mind to. For shame! Forty years I've been working, and such gullible loafers I've never seen. Why did you do this, Shifrin? Answer to the collective!"

What could I say? I was in the wrong.

"I was wrong, Lev Yakovlevich. Blame it on my youth."

"What's youth got to do with it, you recidivist? Now give back right away what you stole from the government."

"I'm sorry, Lev Yakovlevich," I said, "it's already in our plan."

The director sniffed scornfully. "Lovely methods. He steals from the government's right pocket and puts it into the government's left pocket. I'll make mincemeat out of you, Shifrin!"

All in all, I felt wretched.

I got on the bus and saw her immediately. This was the first time I had met her going home. She noticed me —I could feel it—but she didn't tear her eyes away from her damned book.

When we were getting near my stop, I suddenly took her by the hand and pulled her out of the bus. We walked off together.

"Why did you come with me?" I asked.
"I don't know."
"What's the matter with you?"
"I'm scared."
"Come on. What are you scared of?"
"I don't know."
"You're beautiful."
"I want to love."
"Why don't you get married?"
"Silly, I said I wanted to love."
"Love me. I want so badly for someone to love me."

"You have kind eyes."
"Stop laughing at me."
"Really, I mean it."
"Why did you come with me?"
"You have kind eyes. Hey, do you like operettas?"
"Hate them."
"Me too. I want you to be talented."
"What for?"
"I'll help you. You know, you'll write a book, and I'll sit beside you."
"I don't know how to write a book."
"Well, then you'll invent a machine. And I'll draft blueprints for you all night. . . ."
"Silly, I'll never invent a machine."
"Well, then you don't have to. You'll read the newspaper, and I'll look at you. And then you'll go far, far away. . . . And I'll wait. Wait . . . wait . . . and trust. . . . And you'll come home. I'll be standing by the door. And then I'll tuck you in, and I'll look at you while you sleep. . . ."
"Silly. . . ."
"Do you know how awful it is to be waiting all the time?"
"Sure, I know. I'm always waiting myself."
"You won't leave me? Don't leave. Please. I couldn't stand it if you left. . . ."

We didn't say a word to each other. I was afraid she'd say something and ruin the whole thing. But she, too, kept silent.

We went home to my place, and I kissed her. And then I kissed her again, a long kiss. . . . And then she left. . . .

I was as happy as if I had returned to my homeland after a long, long separation. . . .

8

AN OLD MAN named Sidorov worked with me in the quality control division. He was a kind man, exceptionally apathetic towards his work. He didn't give a damn about anything. In the morning he would make his way around the shops, not in any hurry, chew the fat with the workers about how great it was in the good old days and how bad things have gotten today. Then he would go back to the office and spend the whole day entering his observations in the foremen's book. His entries were not distinguished by great variety. He would write: "Machine number one is okay, machine number two is also okay, machine number three is okay . . ." It was a real pleasure to work with old Sidorov.

In the summer he went to Klin, or maybe Kalinin, and there he died.

Everyone in the plant was upset. The director called me into his office and said, "You knew old Sidorov well. I'm assigning you to be chairman of the funeral committee. Go to Klin, or is it maybe Kalinin, and bring back the coffin with old Sidorov's body. We'll lay him out in our meeting room, and after we pay our last respects, we'll bury him at the factory's expense. You get me?"

Here's to Your Health,

I got him, all right, and although I didn't like the idea of bringing back dead old Sidorov, I prepared to carry out the assignment. They gave me a car and three husky young guys, and off I went.

Old man Sidorov lay in the local morgue. This was my first visit to a morgue, and to make matters worse, my guide was a skinny, cynical old fellow—this was the morgue watchman—who wouldn't agree to hand over Sidorov unless he got the usual pint of booze.

"You got a pint?" he asked solemnly, leading me through the morgue. I was scared and sickened.

"Yeah, yeah, sure," I mumbled, eye-balling the local inhabitants, who had ended their earthly existence.

"This here one is yours," said the attendant. "Take 'im."

My young bulls took Sidorov, poor devil, and put him in the coffin we had bought in the funeral supplies store with a government chit. I tried not to look at the old man; I felt ashamed in front of him.

We drove down a lonely highway. The Moscow summer reigned along both sides. We sat on Sidorov's coffin, smoking and thinking about life and death. One of the boys told an old joke: "A Jew was on his deathbed. . . ." I sat and thought, "What is this all about? Why are we born, why do we torment ourselves, torment the people around us, fight, quarrel, produce children, eat, read books, believe in God? What for? Take old Sidorov. He brandished a saber in the Civil War, hacked up Reds and Whites, later he starved, built, tilled the earth. Then he was a director of something or other which he never really figured out. He fell, only to fight his way back up again, because he was poisoned by power and dreamed of getting it back. But he didn't quite make it, because he was primitive and uneducated. And now he's dead. He's lying in this coffin that I'm sitting on, and later we'll change places: a young Sidorov will sit

Comrade Shifrin!

on my coffin telling stories about how a Jew was on his deathbed. What's left of people and after people?"

The factory yard was filled with workers. They had come to pay their last respects to old Sidorov. As we drove into the yard, all conversation stopped and the music started up—our brass band struck up a march. The conductor of the band, Zhorka from the metal shop, came over to me and whispered, without interrupting his conducting, "Tolya, we don't have the sound we need. Kolka, that bastard, got drunk . . . I asked him like a human being, 'Kolka, don't drink tomorrow, we're burying Sidorov. Afterwards do what you like.' But no, that son-of-a-bitch has ruined all my music."

"What instrument did he play?"

"Cymbals!" Zhorka moaned with despair. "Brass cymbals, you know? We would have had boom-chi, boom-chi, just great, but without cymbals it's a joke. . . ."

"Wait a minute," I said. "I'll tell Lev right away."

I made my way to the director and said, "Lev Yakovlevich, there's a problem with the band—there are no cymbals. The cymbals got drunk."

"It's a good thing you didn't get drunk, too," said the director. "Go help this provincial Stokowski. Play the cymbals for him."

"You know," I said, "this is too much. First get Sidorov, now play the cymbals. I'm an engineer, not a jazz musician. Play the cymbals yourself."

"I don't know how," said the director, "or else I'd help out my comrades. It's not such a big deal to play the cymbals. Tell me, you enjoy more to argue with your director than to help out the collective? I've never seen such an undisciplined employee in my life. So go and play, I tell you!"

I cast a vicious glance at the director and went over to Zhora.

"How do you play these idiotic cymbals?"

"Tolya darling," he said with joy, blowing his horn and waving his free hand, "I'll show you. When I go like this, bang the cymbals together, and when I don't go like this, just keep quiet. Okay?"

I picked up the cymbals and joined the band. The people around me started whispering. Zhorka waved his hand, and I banged the cymbals together with force. The band came alive. Everyone began to play more harmoniously and energetically. And I slammed and crashed my cymbals! I listened and banged the cymbals. I didn't see my comrades' faces, didn't see the workers, nor the coffin with old Sidorov, nor the director—I didn't see anything. I was intoxicated with surprise and happiness. Suddenly, I was a creator. I was creating music, and it seemed that the sounds of violins and cellos were being born from beneath my hands. It was I who brought to life the chords of the organ and the growling of the trombones. It was I who composed this Beethoven march as old as the world, as old as old Sidorov! I hit my cymbals and was as free as a song rushing to the mountains. I was a Caucasian horseman, I was a strongman! I could have shouted to all creation: "God! See who I am! I'm also a god! I'm creating! I'm music! I'm. . . ."

Zhorka was looking at me with surprise and cueing me in the right places, and I mentally thanked the director for making me play in this band, made up of boys and old men. And it occurred to me that these boys and old men were certainly not just tooting on their horns, for in these horns I caught sight of another, unknown, life. . . .

Thank you, old Sidorov. Forgive me: you helped me feel happiness. Thanks, old man!

---------9

OUR PRINTING PLANT had staff meetings every Monday. All the supervisors gathered in the director's office and reported on the fulfillment of the plan for the previous week. The director heard them out and gave instructions. Those who were lagging behind were berated in terrible language, and those in the vanguard of production were set against the laggards. The engineers called these meetings "purgatory."

The director had one thing that set him off: he was afraid of fires. In the middle of dressing us down he would stop and sniff the air. He always thought he smelled smoke. So one day after he had said: "Because of you, Surin, the plant is not fulfilling the production plan. I'll beat the hell out of you, Surin! Never in my life have I seen such a stupid paper shop supervisor. Is it just possible, Surin, that you don't know that books are printed on paper?"—he stopped, sniffed the air, and asked, "What's that smell?"

I was sitting in the last row playing a word game with Genka Levin. You know, you pick a word and then make other words using the letters in it. Whoever thinks up the most words wins. I heard the director's question and said automatically, "The factory's burning because of Surin."

Dead silence.

The director pushed a button. Galya came in.

"Get me Davydovsky, make it snappy."

It was very quiet. Two minutes later I looked gloomily out the window and saw Davydovsky, the fire warden, hobbling across the factory yard. He came into the office, straightened up, and barked, "At your service, Lev Yakovlevich!"

"Davydovsky, Shifrin says that our factory is burning. Find out *where* it's burning and report back to me."

"Yes, sir, Lev Yakovlevich," Davydovsky saluted and hurried off to carry out his instructions.

No one said a word. The director looked out the window and drummed his fingers on the glass. Five minutes later Davydovsky returned.

"Nothing's burning anywhere, Lev Yakovlevich."

"Stand up," the director said to me.

I stood up.

"Look at him," said the director. "Do you see this idiot?"

My coworkers looked at me.

"We see him," said Surin.

"Maybe someone is pulling your tongue, Shifrin? Why do you want me to have a heart attack on account of you? Where did you see the factory burning?" The director wouldn't calm down.

"Lev Yakovlevich, I meant in the metaphorical sense. I meant that the factory is burning with zeal to catch up with the plan. That's what I had in mind."

"He 'had in mind!' I'll have you in mind! I'm not even talking about the fact that you've automatically lost your bonus this month for hooligan outbursts in the director's office. More than that, I'm going to ask that they summon you to the Party Bureau. You're a joke, not a human being! Now stand up while your comrades

Comrade Shifrin!

make their reports. Let everyone see what a savage you are!"
 The director was very upset. I felt sorry for him. Standing up, I finished my word game with Genka Levin, won, and whispered to him, "You owe me a cognac." I waited out the meeting, and walked into the yard. My coworkers pressed my hand warmly as they went by, expressing their sympathies as if I were the wife of the deceased. Yurka Surin, the paper-shop boss, slapped me on the back and said, "Your pathetic little sortie was justly punished. Everyone who has ever lifted a hand against the paper shop has perished in fearful agony."
 "Shifrin, report to the director's office," said the secretary Galya, on her way to the cafeteria.
 "My God, what next?" I thought, walking into his office.
 "Well, how did you like your spanking? Not too bad?" the director asked sympathetically.
 "Not too bad. It could have been worse."
 "It certainly could," he agreed. "Sit down, please."
 I didn't like that. The director never said "sit down, please" to anyone. I sat down on the very edge of the chair.
 "You are a young engineer with a degree," the director said pensively. "You must grow. Don't you think so?"
 "I am growing," I said uncertainly.
 "You're growing in the wrong direction," he said. "You're growing in rudeness to your director, that's how you're growing. To waste no words, I'm assigning you to be the supervisor of the printing shop. It will be better that way."
 "What?" I got scared. "It's too soon. I don't have enough experience."
 "We'll help, we'll help you," he said quickly. "You're cut out for better things. If you can talk to the director

Here's to Your Health,

like that at meetings, you'll be able to talk to the workers, too."

So I became the boss of the printing shop. The shop supervisor has to know how to do everything. He has to yell at the foremen, sense the mood in the shop, organize work shifts, assign the work, convince the women not to have abortions, reconcile husbands and wives, fire drunks, teach trainees, stay on good terms with the quota-setters, argue with the bookkeeper, assign people to collective farms to dig potatoes, root out promiscuity, maintain cleanliness, be an auxiliary worker, drink with the senior foreman, and fulfill the plan according to all twelve criteria.

The plan is constructed shrewdly. If you succeed in turning out the required quantities of each type of product—the quantity of output—then you can't achieve the target as defined in monetary terms—the value of output.

"Lev Yakovlevich, how are we going to make our cash target?"

"However you like!"

So you sit up late into the night and wrack your brains —how the hell are we going to make enough money? Finally, it occurs to you: you have to steal it. Steal from the government in order to give back to the government. How to do it? You know that a unit of production costs, say, five kopecks. But if it were to cost eight kopecks, then you could fulfill the plan. It's your job to find these three kopecks. Now, who is the most important person on the premises? No, you didn't guess right. The most important person on the premises is the cost-controller! It is he who holds in his hands the power to fix production prices.

So, you take a little bottle of vodka and go to visit the cost-controller, dear Nikolai Semyonovich.

Comrade Shifrin!

"Nikolai Semyonovich—ardent greetings!" I said cheerfully as I entered his office.

Nikolai Semyonovich looked like an office drudge out of Saltykov-Shchedrin. He was a crafty old man and a great lover of drink.

"How're things going, young man?" he inquired, staring fixedly at my bulging pocket, out of which peeked a bottle secured especially for this visit.

"Eh, not so good," I grieved. "It's hard, Pop, hard. The plan, you know, is a terrible thing. You waste away, you work, raise production, push harder, and still you fall short."

"That's right," he said gravely. "Drink, don't drink—all the same it costs two rubles."

"Exactly," I said, "that's it exactly, dear Nikolai Semyonovich. Maybe you could give young people a hand, eh? Our current production is so complicated! It should be priced in the sixth group, three kopecks higher, eh, Nikolai Semyonovich? Then we would make our target, and you would make your plan. Eh, Nikolai Semyonovich?"

"You know, it might not be so bad! Ooh, my tooth aches something awful.... It draws... I'm suffering like the devil...." He was squinting at the cherished bottle.

"Here, cure your little toothache, Nikolai Semyonovich. The best remedy."

Taking a deep breath, Nikolai Semyonovich hid the bottle in his desk and said, "Leave it to me, by tomorrow morning I'll think of something. I won't sleep all night, I'll be thinking for you, young fellow. Go on. The soldier sleeps, but the army goes on. Drink, don't drink—all the same it costs two rubles. . . ."

A month later the director called me into his office and said, "You're not thinking hard enough, son. You have to use your head, be the brains for your shop. Your work norms are too low. You must bring them up. . . . Think about it. The planning section is increasing your work load. I've given the instructions."

I spoke with the planning section. They proposed increasing the output norms from each machine by seventeen to twenty percent. This meant, in effect, that the salaries of my workers would decrease seventeen to twenty percent.

"So what are we supposed to do?"

"They should be producing more. Increase the speed of the machines. We have to consider labor productivity."

The order to change the output norms was signed. We decided to put it through quietly, without discussion. The next morning, when I reached the entrance to the shop, an uneasy feeling came over me. I didn't hear the accustomed hum of the machines—the shop was not operating. The printing presses were not rolling, the auxiliary workers were not bustling about with their carts filled with printed sheets, the paper sorters weren't rustling through the finished work. The shop was silent as Sunday.

My foremen surrounded me, confused.

"What's going on here?" I asked, heading quickly for the shop office.

"They didn't start work this morning," a pale Foreman Belov informed me. "I tell them, 'To your places right away,' and they say, 'Not until they give us back our old norms!'"

"Get me the Party organizer," I ordered. The workers came in.

"What kind of a Soviet plant is this!?" I said to the Party organizer Orlov, a printer. Orlov, a shrewd, patient guy, lit a cigarette, sat down on the edge of the couch, and said, "It's not right, Tolya. The workers should have been told about the change ahead of time.

Comrade Shifrin!

But you acted so fast—boom! boom! boom!—and it's done. We all have children, families, household budgets. And you're lowering our salaries."

"We're not lowering them, we're evening out the norms."

"Then even them out in the other direction—is this any way to even them out?"

"Look, Orlov," I said, "you yourself understand what this is all about. And you understand what we're threatened with. If the workers don't get to their places in ten minutes, I'll have to fire the printers."

"Tolya, the workers will write a complaint to the Central Committee!"

"Let them write. But I request that they get to work right away."

In walked the director. I saw by his face that he already knew everything.

"Well, well," he began to growl, "here it is the middle of the work day, and Shifrin is holding a meeting. What, did all your machines break down? Maybe you decided to take a rest?"

"No, Lev Yakovlevich," I said. "We had a little misunderstanding here." I looked Orlov in the eye. "But it's already straightened out."

Orlov smiled bitterly, put out his cigarette butt against his heel, and walked out of the shop.

I stood with the director and we overheard the exclamations coming from behind the door.

Orlov's low baritone tried to convince them. "What does Tolya have to do with it? He's a pawn, he did what he was told. Even Lev isn't to blame here."

"And who's to blame, then?" This was Mitka Burlayev, a printer's assistant.

"Ah, the motherfuckers. . . . Let's give notice." This was Spiridonov, the best printer.

71

"And where are we going to go? It's the same everywhere."

"You just get settled in and right away they go and raise the norms. . . ."

"That's okay. We'll write you-know-where, let them take care of it."

"Comrades, we have to get to work. The machines have been idle for two hours already." This was Ivan Ivanovich, the trade-union organizer.

"Better you should be thinking about us, Vanya. Let Tolya worry about the machines. That's what he gets paid for. . . ."

The director and I exchanged glances. There was an ironic twinkle in his eye.

All of a sudden one machine started humming, then a second, and then the whole shop was filled with the usual grinding and rustling. I took a deep breath.

"Not too bad," said the director. "It could have been worse. . . ."

10

IN MOSCOW, youth cafés were the latest craze. The Komsomol regional committee called me in and told me, "You will be the board chairman of the Martians Café." So I became the chairman. I liked the job. First of all, you were meeting people all the time. Secondly, you had someplace to go in the evening. And third, it was an honor, because there were only two youth cafés in Moscow, and you were one of two chairmen. . . .

I had my own little table in the corner. I sat there every evening, giving advice to the Komsomol volunteers, resolving arguments that would arise, and chatting with individual patrons who wanted to know this or that. The band played, lovers danced, and Liusya the barmaid smiled at me from time to time from her post. . . .

One evening a small pack of young men came into the café; there were eight of them. The doorman/coatman, a man with the strange name of Patefonov (Mr. Phonograph), looked sternly after them and said to Lyonya Sinelnikov, a member of the café board, "Keep an eye on them; there's something I don't like about their looks. . . . Okay?"

The young men took a table and opened a suitcase

they had brought with them. It was packed to the top with bottles of cognac.

From my observation post I saw one of them, a pale kid, quickly empty two bottles, pouring a full glass for each of them. The young men grunted, drained their glasses, and immediately poured a second round.

Board-member Lyonya Sinelnikov put on a stern face and confidently approached the transgressors' table.

"Young men," he said, "you are breaking the rules of the Martians Café. I ask you to stop drinking at once and hand over this unfortunate suitcase to our doorman/coatman Patefonov."

"Beat it, creep," was the answer. "Or you'll be sorry. Got that, pal?"

After considering the foregoing, Lyonka said in a more threatening tone, "Very well . . . ," and headed over to my table. I prepared myself for his report.

"Tolya, there are some hooligans sitting over there. They're drinking cognac and they've insulted me. And today I am the board member in charge."

"Good. What do you suggest we do?"

"I suggest we kick them out of our café right away. They're scum," said the insulted Lyonka.

"Okay, tell them we've decided to ask them to leave."

An off-key song rose from the vicinity of the drunken crowd at the table.

Liusya looked reproachfully at me from behind her counter, as if it were my fault that they were howling and ignoring Lyonka's good advice. Feeling my responsibility as a member of the collective, I stood up, went over to their table, and, looking into Pale-face's eyes, I said, "You've been warned, but you didn't listen. In the name of the café board, of which I am the chairman, I ask you to leave our premises."

The fellows at the table laughed, and the pale kid said

Comrade Shifrin!

languidly, "Drop dead. Get away from our table, you asshole, and quit bugging me. . . . The drinks aren't on you, so get the hell out of here."

I looked at him the way in the movies a heavy-weight champion in mufti looks at an egghead who bumps into him on the street, and I mounted the stage.

"Friends," I said into the microphone, addressing the patrons. "Friends, our marvelous café has been invaded this evening by drunken hooligans. They want to spoil our evening. They are disturbing our leisure. And our lives!" And then I added as an afterthought, remembering some newspaper article I had read headlined, "Pull the Weeds from our Soviet Lawn!": "Let's pull the weeds from our Soviet lawn! Surely there are some real men among us who can teach this shameless bunch of hooligans a lesson and kick them out of here. How about it?"

There was some movement in the room. On all sides chairs were pushed back, and here and there loomed the powerful figures of the café's male patrons. They rolled up their sleeves and, amidst a chorus of "Where?" "Who?" and "What's going on?" rushed over to where the suitcase owners were drinking their foolish cognac.

What had I started! The pale kid shouted, "Let's give it to those parasites!" Grabbing a heavy metal chair (modern, the pride of the café), he flung it into the crowd of onrushers. His colleagues quickly joined the exercise. The other patrons roared, "How dare you!" and began to wrestle with the delinquents. But this was just the beginning. The pack took the offensive. Wielding empty bottles, they smashed the bottoms against the table and threw themselves upon the crowd with these frightening weapons of broken glass.

"Mama!" I yelled, realizing that this was my last day on earth.

It was like a good gangster movie: women's bloodcurdling screams, blood, broken dishes littering the floor, cursing and swearing, cries and dull blows.

It went on like a montage: I hear a cry, "To-o-l-ya-a!" I turn around with a shudder. A bottle of champagne is hanging over my head. Someone grabs the arm attached to the champagne, and the bottle breaks against the wall.

In the middle of the room, in the very center of the brawl, a man in a black suit is standing, eating a roasted chicken while the grease runs down his hands. He eats without stopping: only his eyes move, rolling from side to side with pleasure and ecstasy, taking in all the action.

Liusya is hiding behind the bar. Suddenly, just when the air is clear of flying bottles and stools, up she pops like a marionette in front of a screen; deftly, she scoops up the bottles and glasses that have miraculously escaped destruction and sweeps them under the bar. More shouts, wheezes, groans. . . .

I'm screaming, yelling like a madman, "Stop it! We'll kill each other! We're killing each other!"

Lyonka Sinelnikov, his shirt torn and his nose and one eye smashed, shouts into my ear, "Get the police. Hurry up. We'll hold the fort."

"Okay." I run out without my coat onto the frosty January street.

The winter had turned out to be snowy. Snow sparkled in rainbow colors under the street lights. The orange windows of the cooperative apartment house across the street were glowing cozily. There were few passersby. Moscow was going off to sleep. This process is always interesting and amusing. First the stores and public toilets close. This is a hint, so to speak, that there's no reason to hang around on the street. Time to go home to sleep, citizens. The tobacco kiosks and ice cream and soda vendors close up shop. The theater performances end, and the subway waits for the last

Comrade Shifrin!

moviegoers and the workers from the second shift. Then they, too, are gone. There's still a bit of life in the closing restaurants. The last drunks, mumbling and bumming cigarettes from passersby, gather in the empty subway cars to doze off in some soft corner, until the vigilant subway police lead them out to freedom or to the precinct station. And that's it. Moscow is lost in heavy, dreamless sleep. That's it. In the morning, back to work. . . .

I ran, puffing and panting, as fast as I could go, to the police station—after all, people in the Martian Café were killing each other. I ran like Vladimir Kutz when he set his record. I raced straight down the middle of the street, but the passersby looked at me without surprise, because Muscovites are not surprised by anything. How much further—two hundred yards, five hundred? My God! If I could only go faster! I wasn't cold, just soaking wet. At last, the entrance! I burst into the reception area and fell on a bench, too weak to utter a word. Wheezing, using sign language, I tried to explain to an officer in a peaked cap what had happened.

The officer looked at me, his thick-lashed, round black eyes twinkling, and reflectively twirled a key chain.

"Comrade officer," I said, "in the Martians Café . . . hooligans . . . beating up. . . . Hurry, please . . . send some men. . . . It's awful . . . Come on."

The officer stared at me attentively.

"Please, calm yourself," he said. "Try to explain everything clearly. . . ."

But I was already speeding back to the café. I was sure that I'd go in and find the corpse of Lyonya Sinelnikov or Liusya, or something else that I was afraid to even think about. I was on the verge of collapse.

The café entrance was deserted. I burst in, shouting with rage, "Where are they? Now we'll get them!"

77

Here's to Your Health,

The café was empty. Everyone had left. Only a group of my volunteers remained, licking their wounds, gathering together the chairs strewn about the room, righting overturned tables, and mopping up broken glass.

"They left," said Lyonya. "They broke loose, surrounded our doorman/coatman Patefonov, stuck a long knife under his nose, grabbed their coats, and ran."

We sat around as if we had just been through a bombing raid, and stared blankly at the floor.

The door opened and a boy of about sixteen walked in. He glanced around furtively and went over to a chair with a jacket hanging on it.

"Can we do something for you?" I asked without energy.

"I just wanna get my jacket here. I forgot my jacket," he said.

"So take it."

The boy had already retrieved the jacket, when suddenly Liusya said, "Tolya, I think he's one of them. He was sitting at their table...."

"Aha!" we began to roar passionately. "A-a-a! Just who do you think you are! You bandits! What have you done to our wonderful Martian Café? Vandals! Out with it, who were your accomplices?"

"You can cut me to pieces, I won't squeal on them," said our enemy courageously. We had bound him hand and foot.

"So, you won't talk, eh? You'll tell us everything!"

"Never!" said the boy. "Hack me to pieces and still I won't tell!"

Since the police never did arrive, we closed the café and took our prisoner off to the local station house, where, in a matter of minutes, he told us his name and the names of his comrades: they were waiters at a restaurant and had just gotten paid. They felt uncomfortable drinking in their own restaurant, and since they had heard such good things about the Martians Café,

Comrade Shifrin!

they decided to spend some time there, "classy, like." But they couldn't control themselves, and they got drunk right away. And that was the start of the whole mess.

"We're sorry if we did something wrong...."

Later there was a trial. I was the public prosecutor. I angrily attacked drunkenness.

"We have no social reasons for drunkenness," I said. "Which makes the ugly behavior of these thugs all the more shameful. We try, we provide youth with all the conditions for cultured leisure, and these hooligans carry on like our enemies. They are antisocial, and we ask that they be punished...."

My speech made a strong impression on the defendants. I left feeling that I had done my duty....

11

I WAS VERY GREEDY in my youth. I hungrily pursued new sensations, new feelings. I wanted to know right away even those things I would have been better off not knowing. When I was fifteen, I went after love, passionately, enthusiastically, discovering with wonder and amazement the previously closed world of girls. Even earlier I had smoked my first cigarette. And not long after that, I downed my first shotglass of vodka to impress my friends. Gasping and choking, fish-mouthed, I staggered across the yard like a drunk, to the envy of my less experienced peers.

I was in a hurry to get through my youth because I thought it would be more fun to be an adult. To be an adult meant to have an absolute knowledge of everything forbidden. I greedily flared my nostrils and flung myself into the jungles of sensation. When I had gone the whole round of "growing up," I suddenly thought with horror that I had left nothing for "later on." "Life will be dull," I thought, "if I find out everything right this minute." So I made the decision to leave some sensations for "later on." To my shame, very little indeed was left: only the racetrack

Comrade Shifrin!

and the parachute jump remained to be tasted.
Once in the summer my friend Mark and I took a day off together. We walked around sunny, dusty Moscow. For a while we strolled quietly, and then we started fooling around: we walked up to policemen and passersby and asked idiotic questions.
"What more would you need to be happy?" we asked, pulling out our notebooks.
"You," answered the girls we approached.
"Don't bother me," a policeman snapped sternly. "Don't you see this traffic?"
"There isn't enough of anything," middle-aged women said with a sigh.
We didn't bother with men.
I loved Leningrad Highway. Whenever Mark and I came across this road, for some reason, we began to sing in two-part harmony (or so it seemed to us) an old Hussar song:

> Weapons glinting in the sun,
> Sounds of trumpets dashing,
> Raising dust along the road—
> Hussars' eyes are flashing!

And then we roared the refrain:

> Don't you weep, oh, don't you mourn,
> My darling . . .

The passersby were not surprised, because Muscovites are never surprised by anything. And on that day off, as we finished howling the last verse—

> Nine months later to the day,
> White arms rock and gently sway

Here's to Your Health,

What her blue eyes gaze upon—
Gallant Hussar's little son . . .

—we found ourselves in front of a large, stately structure with wrought-iron horses above the portico. This was the racetrack.

"You can't escape from fate," I said, taking a deep breath. "Let's go, my friend, here we are at the races. One less sensation for 'later on.'"

"Nothing doing," said Mark, "we are Soviet men, with iron wills. We shouldn't take part in this bourgeois orgy. Wives wait in agony for husbands who waste away their lives at the races. Happiness is but a shadow to the wife who vainly awaits her husband's pay envelope. . . ."

"But we're bachelors," I said curtly, and this decided the matter.

We bought tickets for twenty kopecks and went through the gate.

The racetrack was a world unto itself. The people there were a completely different breed. They stood in groups and spoke a strange, twittering language: "Two, twenty-three, four hundred, the first race, seventh position. . . . Let's put down a deuce on this one. . . ." Some walked slowly in front of the long row of cashiers' windows set behind a wall of chicken-wire, studying the faces of the other betting customers.

The races had not yet begun. We bought programs and began loudly to discuss the good and bad points of each horse and jockey. We didn't know anything, but we were talking very confidently. Soon, a small crowd of disreputable racetrack habitués had gathered around us, giving their advice and commenting on the odds.

This was the betting procedure: seven horses ran in

Comrade Shifrin!

each race. If you put money on some horse and it finished first, then you could win as much as five rubles. And if you bet on a combination, putting money on two horses in two races, then—wow!—think how much you could win!

All this was explained to us by a shabby little man whose talk indicated that he was an old hand at the horses. "Bet on this one and this one," he tapped the betting sheet with his finger. "If you win, give me a commission for the advice."

"I have my own ideas," I announced. "I would rather bet on *these* two nice horses and win on my own."

Mark said, "Leave him alone, citizen! Let this pathetic dilettante be responsible for himself. Give him the opportunity to lose his money. Let him lose the hard way."

I said, "I want to bet on Scout in the first race and Vega in the second."

The shabby man wrinkled his face like a pear left over from last year's harvest, and, looking at me with disgust, said to Mark, "Listen, man, this tall guy here, he don't know his ass from his elbow and wants to lose on purpose. But you, you're a serious fellow, don't let him be so stupid as to bet on Scout—in the last three years he hasn't done any better than sixth place. And as for Vega—that's just ridiculous. The jockey is second-rate, he doesn't know how to ride. Tell him, man . . ."

I said, "Stranger, you are absolutely wrong. A horse with a name like Scout can't help but win. He's called Scout precisely because he's the first to succeed, demoralizing the enemy. As for Vega—you don't have a trace of the romantic in you. For me, Vega personifies the successes of man in space. Don't you read the newspapers, sitting here at this lousy racetrack? Don't you know that Vega is one of the zero-magnitude stars, second in brightness only to Sirius? In the not-too-distant future a Soviet man will be the first to step precisely on this star. I emphasize—the first! For this reason I'm betting on Vega. As for the second-class jockey, that's even better. He most certainly wants to become first-class, while a first-class jockey has nothing to strive for, and so might well come in second."

It seemed to me that I convinced him, because he spit and quietly walked away without looking back.

I went up to a window to buy a ticket.

"Excuse me," I said to the middle-aged woman cashier, "I'd like to put a ruble on two horses I've picked. And sell me a ticket for a seat in the grandstand."

"No, young man," said the cashier, "I won't sell you a ticket."

"Why not?" I asked with astonishment.

"This is your first time in this dump, and I don't want you to gamble. You'll lose your shirt."

"What is this?" I yelled. "I want to bet on a horse! The law's on my side. Give me a ticket right now! I won't lose my shirt, I swear! The race is starting, give me a ticket, hurry up! I'll file a complaint!"

"Young man," the cashier said sadly, "this isn't the first five-year plan I've sat through at this place. I've seen a whole constellation of respectable people pass by this window and ruin themselves gambling. Do you know what gambling is?"

"No," I said. "I don't know what gambling is, but I want to find out in the worst way. And I won't let you stop me. Take my ruble, madame, and give me a ticket on Vega and Scout."

"Very well," she said, "I'll sell you a ticket on one condition: if you lose, you go home right away."

"Yes, yes, I swear I'll go home right away."

"Did you hear him promise?" the cashier asked Mark.

"Yes," said Mark, "we'll leave right away."

Comrade Shifrin!

"Hurry up and bet," I said to Mark, "or they'll start without us."

"No," he answered. "I never tempt fate. I'm going to be just an ordinary, intelligent spectator."

We got to the grandstand just as the race was beginning. Beautiful, strong horses fidgeted at the starting post. They were harnessed to tiny carts in which the jockeys sat. The latter wore peaked caps and colorful shirts—orange, white, blue, red, with large checks. They looked like festive toys. Each jockey wore a number. Scout was driven by number six. The signal sounded, and a little Moskvich drove out onto the track, with wing-like barriers attached to either side of it. This was the starting car. The jockeys lined up behind the barriers. A hush came over the track. Start! They're off! Scout, a glossy brown stallion, waved his hooves ridiculously, stamped about, and instantly fell behind. My protegé—the second-class jockey—made some hand movement that I didn't catch, and Scout lunged ahead full speed to overtake the rest of the herd. I gave a yell.

Actually, I yelled in vain. I knew very well that my horses would win. In the first place, I had beginner's luck. And in the second place, I'm always lucky exactly where I don't need it. In short, my horses came in first. It happened this way:

"Come on, Scout, little spy, little agent—run for your life! Give it all you've got!" I screamed.

Scout heard me. As he flew past me, he turned his head and winked. I calmed down.

"This is just a formality," I said to Mark. "He's going to come in first."

"Don't be a fool," said Mark. The horses thundered towards the finish line, accompanied by the shrieks of the crowd.

"The winner is—Scout," said the loudspeaker.

Here's to Your Health,

My neighbors in the grandstand were staring at me. I was smiling calmly, like an idiot. My neighbors turned away.

"Let's go get our money," I said to Mark.

"It was a mistake to play a combination," Mark said. "It's completely improbable that you'll win the second race, too. And they don't pay up for just one horse. So this doesn't even count."

Between races I pestered my neighbors like Absalom Iznurenkov in Ilf and Petrov's novel, *The Twelve Chairs*.

"They are magnificent horses, aren't they?" I asked a hollow-cheeked tout in a torn raincoat.

"Huh?" he snarled.

"Tell me, please, how fast can a horse go at full speed?" I asked a guy who was spitting and "motherfucking" after every other word. He regaled his comrades: "So and so—bitch, bastard—he, the rotting corpse—won—the louse—last night—motherfucker—in the seventh—son-of-a-bitch—race." While he filled me in on the speed characteristics of native stallions, I thought about how we live a really strange, absurd life. What the hell was I doing here wasting my precious time? And how sad it was to fool around all the time.

I thought about how I was already twenty-five years old and still hadn't done anything with my life. About how the only thing I had learned was to keep quiet at staff meetings. How our life was like these races. Only we didn't sit in the carts and drive the horses—we were the ones who were driven. Someone we didn't see drove us with a strong and capable hand. We just raced madly towards the finish line, not understanding why. We flew pointlessly around in a circle, trying to get ahead of the rival at our side, while the grandstand watched with pity and passion, whistling and shrieking. Afterwards, we would go into our stalls, and grooms in

Comrade Shifrin!

white robes would bring us oats. The one who came in first would probably get an extra ration of oats and a few slaps on his glossy, sweating sides. And then we would talk about our achievements, our vacations at rest homes, about the movie *The Magnificent Seven*, about the blonde in the first row. And we would listen and chew our oats, glancing sideways into our neighbor's stall. And then, full and satisfied, we'd gather into herds and recall those thrilling days of yesteryear when we were wild, swift, and unbroken. How we ran freely and easily across our prairies, how the air rang with the inviting neighs of the young chestnut mares, how sweet and pure was the water that ran through White Mist Canyon. How wonderful it would be to tear out of our dingy stalls and race around Moscow, ignoring traffic lights and forcing pedestrians to cling with fright to the sides of buildings. And the next day they'd lead us out again to the cinder track. Run . . . , run. . . .

The second race began. I looked at Mark and understood why he hadn't bet—he was afraid of winning.

Vega was running under number one. I watched apathetically as she broke ahead and easily galloped first across the finish line.

"The winner is—Vega!" came the passionless announcement.

Mark looked at me silently.

"Let's go," I said. "The game is over."

We went up to the cashier.

"Madame," I said, "I won."

"I knew it," she said. "You unlucky man."

"Why am I unlucky?"

"Because now you'll never leave here. Winning is fatal to novices."

"I gave my word," I said. "We're leaving this den of iniquity right away."

"I'd be glad . . ." And I believed that she was sincere.

Here's to Your Health,

I took my forty-five rubles in winnings and walked towards the exit. The shabby little man came up to me and said, "See? I told you . . ."

I gave him a ruble.

"Good-bye, sir. Never give advice to professional gamblers."

He looked at me with respect and silently walked away.

Mark and I emerged into the light of day on sunny Racetrack Street.

"Mark, this filthy, free money is burning my hand. We've got to get rid of it right away. I propose we drink it up this very second."

"Done," he said.

We went into the Racing Restaurant and sat down at a table.

A waiter hurried over to us.

"What would you like?" he asked, suddenly giving us a strange look.

"This, this, and this," I ordered.

"And this," added Mark.

"And this too," I specified, "and two bottles of your very best cognac."

"And a little cup of coffee," Mark summed up.

When we had drunk and eaten, I looked around the room and suddenly felt a certain tension in the air. The waiters were running over to each other, whispering back and forth, pointing out our table with their eyes. When my gaze met one of theirs, they turned away immediately.

"Will there be anything else?" asked our waiter. I looked up and recognized him. He was one of the hooligans from the Martians Café incident. And so were all the other waiters. They had recognized me right away, and were waiting for me to get drunk.

Comrade Shifrin!

"That's all for now," I said to the chap, looking him straight in the eye.

"Mark," I whispered into my friend's ear, "I'm very, very drunk, but I absolutely, *absolutely* cannot be drunk now. We must act like gentlemen. I'll explain later."

I sobered up. I had never been so sober in my life.

"Good day," I said to the waiter.

"Hello," he said softly. "Did you come looking for me?"

I saw fear in his eyes. How repulsive—he was afraid of me! There was no getting around it: I would always have to be the boss of the Martians Café. I had since left the post of chairman, but in his eyes I would play that role forever.

"No," I said, "I didn't come looking for you. I came into your bar to show you how much a man can drink and still remain sober, and not lose face, not behave like a hooligan, not break dishes and beat people. But be a human being."

During this monologue I felt like a vile hypocrite, because I was drunk, because I was lying, because I felt my superiority over this kid, because the law was on the side of my two-faced respectability—and this guy could do nothing about my stinking demagogy.

"And, what is more," I continued, "I brought my friend here so he could see how you're behaving now, to see if you feel sorry for your wrong-doing. Right, Colonel?"

Mark didn't say a word.

"But it happened that . . . ," said the kid.

"'Happened,'" I mimicked. "What a clown! How much do we owe?"

"Forty-five rubles and thirty kopecks," he whispered, completely stunned.

We paid and left.

"Mark, I'm drunk as a dog. Hold me up, I'm going to collapse," I mumbled. We had managed to walk out of the restaurant with a firm, confident stride, but dropped that act as soon as we had rounded the corner.

I put my arm around my friend's shoulder and we shouted to all Moscow:

> Weapons glinting in the sun,
> Sounds of trumpets dashing,
> Raising dust along the road—
> Hussars' eyes are flashing . . .

And the passersby weren't surprised, because Muscovites are never surprised at anything.

Now all I had left for "later on" was the parachutes. Well, someday I'd get around to making that jump. . . .

12

I HAD ALREADY been working for four years. I had come to love my printing plant, and had gotten used to my comrades. Common misfortune—the plan—had drawn us all together. We all turned on one wheel, in one rhythm. The thirty-first day of one month was exactly like the first day of the next. We knew one thing: each day we had to produce a certain number of rubles' worth of goods, as well as a specified number of products. We boasted to one another of numbers and percentages. We increased labor productivity and lowered the cost of production. We introduced new technology and exchanged curses with the metalworkers. And suddenly, I lost heart.

I longed for another world. I wanted clean collars and attractive ties. I wanted a job without pressure, with no responsibility, and interesting conversations about literature and art. I was tired of fulfilling the plan. It happens. I said to myself, in order to lead an interesting life, I should change my profession every four years. Then I'd see new people, I'd have varied interests, I'd have something to tell my children and grandchildren.

Here's to Your Health,

... I'm sitting in an armchair, my legs covered with a blanket. My hair has turned silver. My grandchildren sit around me. "Grandpa, tell us what you did when you were young."

"Ah, children," I say, "I led a life full of marvelous adventures and unusual encounters. Look at these photographs. Here I am with Lev Yakovlevich. He was my first teacher and boss. He was an unrefined man but wise. He burned with zeal for work and demanded that we burn, too. He made us fall in love with our work, and made us understand that work is the main thing. He was violent and uncouth, but he was a *mensch*.

"He died on the job. He would yell at someone, and then suddenly fall silent. We didn't like it when he was silent. But then one time he was silent forever. He died. I made a speech over his grave. I said that this man's tumultuous life hadn't passed without a trace: he lives on. I read these verses:

> The stonemason places a stone here,
> Lovers pass in the dark. . . .
> Who's alive—lives, who's dead—likewise,
> Some live in houses, others in books. . . .

Lev Yakovlevich lives in the volumes of children's books to which he devoted his life. Take off your hats —a real human being has died!

"And this is a picture of the poet Mikhail Svetlov— that means 'bright.' He really was a radiant man. All his life he did justice to his name. He was always drunk, jolly, and wise. Everyone loved him. Only very bad people didn't like Svetlov. Very bad. His jokes and sayings passed from mouth to mouth and turned into folklore.

Comrade Shifrin!

"'Mikhail Arkadievich,' I once asked him, 'Is it true that you composed this verse about the cosmonaut?'

> Lucky thing that Yu. Gagarin's
> Not a Jew and not Tartarin,
> Neither Tungus nor Uzbek,
> But one of us—a good Soviet!

"He thought a moment and then said, 'No, I didn't compose that. God knows *what* everyone attributes to me. In my life I've written only one epigram. And not even an epigram, but an inscription over a whorehouse —"No pay, no play." '

"Once I got a phone call. An unfamiliar voice said, 'What's the matter with you, you louse? Svetlov is lying close to death, the old man is fading fast, and not one wretch goes to help him. They could at least buy him some food, the bastards.'

" 'Who is this?'

" 'It's me.'

"He hung up.

"Upset, I dialed Svetlov's number.

" 'What can I do for you?' said the familiar guttural voice. 'What is it?'

" 'What's the matter with you, Mikhail Arkadievich? Are you sick?'

" 'Of course, I'm sick. Who's healthy nowadays?'

" 'Maybe I can do something for you?'

" 'What can *you* do? Hey, you!' he yelled to someone in the room. 'Don't you dare clear away that mess! That's my mess!'

" 'Well, as long as you're yelling like that, I know everything's all right,' I said. 'So, you don't need anything?'

"'What do I need?' He thought about it and said, 'I need a refrigerator!'

"'What do you need a refrigerator for?' I said, surprised.

"He said in a whisper, but distinctly, 'So I'd have someplace to cool my hot temper.'

"I imagined his famous Voltaire smile. 'Okay. I'll get you a refrigerator.'

"I hung up and heartily regretted that I had said those words. Where was I going to get him a refrigerator?

"'Girls, where can I buy a refrigerator?' I asked my coworkers.

"'Are you crazy, Tolya?' chirped the girls. 'What do you mean? You have to wait three or four years for a refrigerator. There's a waiting list, and then they check if you really need it. . . . What's wrong with you? It's impossible.'

"'Thanks,' I said. I picked up the phone and called the Minister of Trade. 'It's an urgent matter,' I told the secretary.

"'Comrade Minister, I beg you, help me get a refrigerator for the great Soviet poet Mikhail Svetlov.'

"'You're out of your mind!'

"'Comrade Minister,' I said, 'Mikhail Svetlov, the pride of Soviet poetry, is really a lonely old man. He has no one to look after him, his food is spoiling. Give him a refrigerator, you'll be doing a service to all of Soviet literature.'

"'Who is this Svetlov?'

"'Kakhovka, Kakhovka, our own native rifle . . .' I began to declaim into the telephone.

"'Ah!' recalled the minister. 'That Svetlov?'

"'*That* Svetlov.' I assured him.

"'Okay, call my assistant. I'll give the orders.'

"That refrigerator cost me my health! I called assist-

Comrade Shifrin!

ants and deputies, governing boards and stores. This was no simple matter. It went the round of the entire government apparatus. Finally, in desperation, I phoned the board of the ministry.
" 'What do you want, Comrade?' the angry deputy asked me.
" 'I'm calling about Svetlov's refrigerator,' I said timidly.
" 'Oh, yes, they told me something about it,' he remembered. 'I'll put the question to the board right away . . . Comrades, they're calling about a refrigerator for the poet Svetlov. There's a motion on the floor to sell him a refrigerator. All those against? . . . The question is resolved, Comrade!'
"I phoned Svetlov. 'Do you have the money for the refrigerator?' I asked him.
" 'What refrigerator?'
" 'The one to keep your memory fresh in!' I said with venom.
" 'My boy, you really got me a refrigerator? You poor thing! Well, never mind. I'll dedicate a little poem to you.'
"I delivered his sparkling Lenin refrigerator, but he never got around to dedicating a poem to me. He was very ill. He died in a leap year.

"And see this photograph, children? This is the American writer John Steinbeck. He looked like a lumberjack. He had a beard, and peered at the world through one eye. He opened the other eye only on exceptional occasions.
"He once met with a group of young writers and asked them, 'How goes the struggle, you young wolves?'
" 'With whom?' The young cubs didn't understand.

Here's to Your Health,

"'With everything!' he snapped, without opening his second eye.

"'Hmmm.' The young writers became embarrassed. They were afraid either to lie or not to lie. Young Aksyonov said, 'Hmmm'; young Yevtushenko said, 'Hmmm'; they all said, 'Hmmm.' Only young Akhmadulina said, 'Dear Maître, don't think we're such fools that we can't answer your sincere question. But, mind you, what's really on our minds is something different. Yesterday I was driving my car, and a policeman took away my license. He said that because I was disobeying the traffic rules, I had forfeited my rights—to drive. Now, the only thing that's on my mind is how to get my rights back.'

"'I understand you perfectly!' Steinbeck exclaimed, opening his other eye. 'You're an exceptionally interesting person to talk to, Miss!'

"So, children," I'll tell my granchildren, "I lived an interesting and varied life, which I also wish for you. You must work hard in school and get A's and B's."

. . . It might be like that, I thought, if I changed jobs. I must change my job. Recently there was a show trial in our city. They were trying a poet because he worked nowhere and wrote poems. Strange poems. In his twenty-two years, this poet had succeeded in working in nine places: in a factory, as a longshoreman, on a scientific expedition, and so on. He said that he was studying life. Then the public prosecutor stood up and asked, "What kind of person are you? You're a parasite! I've worked in one place for forty-five years. I'm not a rolling stone, and I'm proud of it!"

I felt terribly sorry for this man. Just think—forty-five years on one job! How could he keep from going out of his mind, poor man?

So I decided to leave the plant. I gave notice and went to say good-bye to the collective.

13

I WENT TO WORK in a publishing house. I was an important boss, in charge of a dozen printing plants in various cities around the country. It was my job to telephone the directors and ask them, "Well, how's the plan? When are you bringing out our books?"

They were supposed to answer, "The plan's okay, so-so. Your books will be out on time."

I was supposed to say, "Well, then, comrade, in that case . . . That's not bad. Good luck!"

They were supposed to answer, "Good-bye, comrade!"

As you see, everything was great. Let sleeping dogs lie. As our cost-controller Nikolai Semyonovich used to say, "The soldier sleeps, but the army goes on." After that looney bin of a printing plant, this was a nice, respectable sanatorium. I rested. Work here ended promptly at five. At three-thirty all the workers would start getting ready to go home. The ladies put on lipstick, powdered their noses, and combed their hair, and the men smoked in the corridors and discussed the latest soccer scores. At five minutes to five, the homeward procession started down all the staircases of the publishing house. The workers piled up at the main door, which the boss of the personnel office held closed with her body. In her left hand she held a stop-watch, and, in her right, a bell. At five on the dot, like a referee on a playing field, she blew the final whistle, so to speak. Her bell informed us that we could leave, and we streamed out to freedom. . . . See, how simple and nice. But after three weeks this kind of life began to be depressing. I was getting bored. I started looking for things to do to pass the work day.

Our publishing house, to use the language of the forties, was the largest in the world. At every meeting the management would say, "Our publishing house, the largest in the world, must . . . " And, in truth, we *were* more than six hundred employees.

Lev Yakovlevich had taught me how to work quickly. "One leg here, the other—there," he used to say, "and woe to him who does it wrong." So that became my habit. At the new job, I finished all my assignments for the whole day in the first forty minutes. Then the rest of the time I fooled around with the other five hundred ninety-nine employees.

This did not please some people. That is, they didn't like the fact that I finished all my work in forty minutes. There were seven of us working in one room. Five women getting ready to retire on pension, myself, and Vitya Shikunov, a fellow my age, a great guy, whose favorite phrase was, "For heaven's sake, don't pay any attention to them." First thing in the morning, the women would start discussing whether or not to open the window. There were five of them, and those who pleaded for it to be opened-or-else-they-would-suffocate were always in the minority. The majority argued thus: "Open it in your own house! We're sitting in enough of a draft here already. Nothing's going to happen to you!" Vitya and I didn't participate in these battles, as they lasted until lunch, and we had other things to chat about.

Comrade Shifrin!

Once, one of the women took me aside and said, "Tolya, you have to understand that it's impossible to work at such a crazy tempo. You're undermining us, Tolya. We've worked a long time in this publishing house, and we know how things must be done. Evidently, you haven't given the matter much thought." I got very angry and even yelled at her. She said quietly, "Ah, dear boy, you don't understand a thing. We're sick, nervous women. It's hard for us, but you . . . " I started to feel sorry for them.

I began to think, what would happen to the publishing house if I were its boss? I would fire two-thirds of the workers, double the salary of the remaining third, and then this third could turn out all the work calmly and efficiently. True, I thought, this would lead to unemployment, and our society has no unemployment. What can you do? Oh, the hell with it. Let things stay the way they are.

I shared these thoughts with Vitya, and he said, "For heaven's sake, don't pay any attention to them." We went to lunch.

After lunch we had a meeting.

I winked at Vitka and asked for the floor.

"Comrades," I said, "all over the country people are taking labor initiatives. Front-rank workers in all sectors are introducing their proposals. So far, there has been none of this in our publishing house. I am introducing a proposal: I'll take on the work of five of my comrades in the unit, and pledge to fulfill it during my work time. I challenge workers in other units to compete with me."

I sat down. Vitya Shikunov applauded modestly. The ladies looked at me with hatred. I jutted out my lower jaw and looked like the superman on the popular poster, "Put Your Money in a Savings Account."

"Hmm," said Comrade Zhelezkin, my supervisor. "An interesting proposal, Shifrin. Ve-e-e-ry interesting.

Here's to Your Health,

And what will happen to the comrades whose work you've taken on?"

"Don't you see, Ivan Vasilievich," I said, "that's the cruel march of progress. The machine forced out the craftsman, automation replaces workers, cybernetics will do away with work altogether. I'm only a tiny screw, so to speak, in the general progress. You catch on, Ivan Vasilievich?"

Zhelezkin loved to chat with me. He was a general in the reserves. When they sent him over to be our boss, it was a holiday for Vitka and me. For a long time there had been rumors whispered around the publishing house that the new boss would be a general. And when he showed up on the staircase in his epaulets, with all his decorations and medals jingling like church bells at Easter, my delight got the better of me. I walked around him, ooh-ing and aah-ing, tsk-ing, wagging my head. I finally said, "Excuse me, Your Excellency. Please never wear civilian clothes to work. Since childhood I've had a craving to serve under the direction of a 'Your Excellency.' Civilian clothes would somehow dampen our zeal, and that, in turn, would be reflected in our work."

"Who are you?" asked the general.

"Just rank-and-file Private Shifrin, Your Excellency," I rapped out in military fashion.

"Come into my office, Shifrin."

I went in. Vitka waited outside the door, dying of laughter and fright.

"You're a smooth talker," said the general. "But why are you calling me 'Your Excellency'? You want me to take offense?"

"No sir, Ivan Vasilievich," I said seriously. "According to the old tsarist system of service ranks, the director of our publishing house should be 'Your Highness'; you, as his deputy, are 'Your Excellency'; I, as your assistant, am 'Your Grace'; and Vitka Shikunov is 'Your

Comrade Shifrin!

Honor'—since it's all the same to him."
"A real joker, you are," said the general, "but, all right, the hell with it, just watch out you don't disgrace me in public, or I'll have your head. And drop in from time to time, we'll chat. You're a smooth talker."
He was a great guy. He came into our office every morning. I would jump up and report, "Your Excellency, everything's just as it was. Too bad, we haven't lost anything."
We were pleased with one another.
"So, that's what you call progress, is it?" he said to me at the meeting. "It would be progress if you would say something sensible—anyone can wag his tongue like that!"
"What do you mean, wag his tongue?" I was offended. "I'm being serious."
" 'Serious,' " he mimicked, "I'll teach you to be serious. Look at your comrades and think about your behavior."
I looked at my ladies. They sat with lips pressed tight, staring at the floor.
And again I felt sorry for them.
"I take back my ridiculous proposal," I said. "This isn't the place for it. . . ."

14

THE SOKOLNIKI EXPOSITION Grounds were black with people. America was demonstrating her successes in industry, agriculture, and the arts. Moscow had never seen such a stir before.

We were wandering around the avenues of Sokolniki for the fifth day. Five days earlier, the secretary of the Party committee had summoned Vitka Shikunov and me, along with some others from the publishing house. "You're going to Sokolniki for five days to visit the pavilions. The organizers of this exposition think we are a country of louts who will fall for their rags and fancy cars. You must prove that this isn't so. For instance, what kind of health care do we have?"

"Free of charge!" I said.

"Right, Comrade Shifrin. And what kind do they have?"

"They have to pay," I said.

"See what kind of argument we have on our side? Go ahead, comrades, and hold our banner aloft. We're not any worse than America—we're better!"

And so I was the expert on health care.

I sat in the last row of the "Question and Answer Club." A girl who spoke Russian well was answering the

Comrade Shifrin!

visitors' questions. They were all alike: "How much does a worker earn? How much does a pair of shoes cost? What is the price of an automobile?" The girl explained patiently. From time to time, I would stand up and ask, "Tell us, what kind of health care do you have—is it free, or do you have to pay?"

"We have to pay."

"So, there. Look at that!" I would say triumphantly, and look victoriously around the room. Then I would sit down.

The girl explained in detail the price of a visit to the doctor, and the costs of injections and medication. I smugly nodded my head. When I raised my hand for the tenth time to ask what kind of health care system they had, free or paid, the girl smiled shrewdly and said, "You probably want to ask what kind of health care system we have—free or paid? For the tenth time, I'll gladly answer you...."

I was put to shame.

Then they switched me to the women's clothing and lingerie pavilion. When our women saw the underwear from overseas, they rolled their eyes and ooh-ed and aah-ed, looking knowingly at one another and nodding significantly.

"Just think," I said, "they're showing off as if they'd never seen underwear.... Underwear is underwear!"

The women pursed their lips and turned away from me contemptuously. One of them whispered, "My God, what underwear!" I was at the ready:

"So what, what's so great about that underwear? It's just underwear. Is ours any worse?"

"Worse?!" one of them screamed, almost in tears. "Look! Look!" She lifted the hem of her skirt. The other visitors were just rolling with laughter.

I turned red and felt like a worm.

"So, how's your argument going?" Vitka Shikunov asked as he passed by. I spit at the perfume display and went off to browse around the malls.

Besides, I had a rendezvous with Tanya. We wandered together under the fragile gold of Sokolniki's foliage and laughed at my adventures at the exposition. Suddenly a husky youth in white tennis shoes popped out from behind a tree and headed straight for Tanya. He was drunk as a son-of-a-bitch and strong as a bull. He grabbed Tanya by the arm and, leaving no doubt as to his intentions, dragged her behind him into the bushes. He couldn't have cared less about me. Poor Tanya broke loose and screamed, "How dare you, you scoundrel?!" The fellow mooed endearingly and began to repeat the maneuver. It was my turn. I shoved him away from Tanya and punched him in the stomach. It made no impression at all. I swung around, and would probably have given him one in the neck, if I hadn't missed. He grabbed me by the tie and began to roar, "I'll kill you, you bastard!" I knew that if he hit me, I'd never get up again.

I: "Why are you pestering her?"

He: "I'll kill you, you son-of-a-bitch!"

I: "Do you want me to haul you off to the police, you hooligan?"

The devil I'd haul him off! He'd haul *me* off wherever he liked. Those weren't hands, they were vises.

He: "I'm going to finish you off right now!"

I: "Get lost, get out of my sight! I'll make hamburger out of you!"

What could I do? Grab Tanya and run away? But she'd hate me forever. What kind of man was I?

A crowd was gathering. Out of the corner of my eye, I saw an indignant old-age pensioner, a girl selling pastries, a boy about fifteen years old. . . . All of them were animatedly discussing the incident.

"Comrade," I said with as much dignity as I could muster, turning to the pensioner, "Please, do me a favor, get a policeman."

Comrade Shifrin!

My adversary fell on me like a truck. I couldn't even move a finger. At last a policeman showed up.

"Break it up!" the cop said, pulling us apart.

I patted myself tentatively—it seemed nothing was broken.

"Tanya," I said cheerfully, "step aside. I'm going to give this gangster five or seven years, and then we'll go on with our stroll."

"Your papers!" the policeman said sternly.

The crowd came to life.

"How dreadful!" wailed the pastry vendor. "People can't even walk in the park in peace. There are hooligans everywhere. . . ."

"I saw with my own eyes," the boy was talking fast, "this one comes along, and her, too, then this one comes over, bam! and this one. . . ."

"I'm a Party member since sixteen hundred and . . . ," said the pensioner. "I've dedicated the rest of my life to the struggle against disturbers of the peace. I saw how this hooligan . . ."

The fellow looked dully at me and said, "Grab *him*. He tried to pick my pocket."

"What?!" I exploded. "Tie him up, Comrade. Do you hear this provocateur? How low can he stoop?"

More police arrived. They grabbed the youth in the white tennis shoes and took him off to the stationhouse. We followed them. Apparently, it hurt the kid to walk with his arms twisted behind him, because he swore and yelled.

As we approached the stationhouse, he suddenly shut up, worked up a whole mouthful of saliva, and spit in the face of one of the policemen. We gasped.

"Why on earth did you do that, you fool?!" I said. "You must be out of your mind!"

The policeman wiped his face, looked dourly at the kid, and said curtly, "That I won't forgive."

We related the essence of the conflict to the officer on

duty. He wrote everything down. He wrote down about the pensioner, a Party member since the seventeenth century, who . . . , and the pastry vendor who interrupted her business in the name of the triumph of justice, and the fast-talking boy who told how this one was walking along, and that one, too, and then this one jumps out. . . .

Several months later I was summoned to appear in court. The kid in the white tennis shoes was on trial.

"Don't go there alone," my friends advised. "There'll be a whole pack of them. He'll be put in jail, and the others will get even with you." I took Vitka Shikunov and went to court.

In the waiting room, a gray-haired, modestly dressed old woman walked up to me.

"What did you do to my Vaska?" she sobbed. "Now they'll put him in jail. My baby, my only son, my breadwinner."

She wept bitterly. Some other women put their arms around her and led her away into a corner, where, crying and contradicting herself, she told what a good boy Vaska was, how he was quiet and never drank, how he wouldn't hurt a fly, and now what misfortune had befallen him, his first payday, and all. . . . And they gave him a fine. . . . Oh, God! What vodka will do. . . . And he's not guilty, Vaska isn't . . .

The women gasped and tsk-ed sympathetically, and I felt like the biggest s.o.b. on earth.

I imagined my mama in this old woman's place, and knew what horror Vaska must have felt when he had sobered up.

In the courtroom I hemmed and hawed, and made excuses for this Vaska. But they gave him time all the same. He shouldn't have spit in that policeman's face.

Vaska kept repeating dully, "I drank vodka . . . I got drunk. . . ."

Comrade Shifrin!

When they took him away, his hair cut and his spirit broken, he said, "Mamochka, forgive me, Mamochka. I was just trying to have a good time, and look what happened. I was bored. . . . Forgive me, Mama. . . ."
A lump formed in my throat. Why is it so boring, I thought, so boring. . . .

15

I REALLY LOVED the border guards. Border guards looked down at us from all the wall posters. They were dressed in tunics with green epaulets and green service caps, and had rifles slung across their backs. One hand held a revolver, while the other shielded keen eyes from the scorching rays of the sun as they peered vigilantly into the distance to search out the enemy. Lying next to the border guard was his trusty friend—a German shepherd with intelligent eyes and stuck-out tongue. Rest assured, comrades, the enemy will not get through! Our border is in capable hands, it's locked up tight!

The movie theaters were showing films about spies. These cunning bastards (always played by the actors Fait and Kulakov) crept across the border in order to blow up our cities and villages, or kill famous scientists, who were always old and absent-minded. These silly scientists always took their secrets home or to their dachas, and it was right there that the spies stole or photographed their blueprints. And we boys waited with sinking hearts—when, oh when, will the strong, handsome border guard appear and expose the enemy? He appeared at the crucial moment, punched the spy

Comrade Shifrin!

in the nose, and tied him up. The limousine of the secret police was already parked in the garden, ready to take the unmasked enemy off to the Lubianka Prison.

I loved Border Guard Maremukha the best. He and his faithful dog Hindu patrolled a section of the southern frontier. Just imagine, Maremukha and Hindu had apprehended more than four hundred border violators! I read about this in books and heard about it on the radio. I liked brave Maremukha. I knew for sure that he would never let fascists on our soil. Just let them try to sneak in!

If Maremukha alone—or, rather, together with his trusty Hindu—rendered harmless more than four hundred spies and saboteurs, then his comrades along the frontier were probably no slouches either! They must have stopped, well, maybe not four hundred, but two hundred enemies apiece. And how many such border guards were there on all the frontiers of our great country! So, fascists and samurai, shake with terror in your lairs, you'll never see even a single inch of our land, and all your cunning schemes will come to nought!

The movies also showed documentary footage: here's the border violator in his quilted jacket, making his way through a dense thicket. Crack! You can hear the faintest snap of a branch. From his hiding place, Maremukha has caught sight of the enemy. But the enemy doesn't suspect a thing. Maremukha picks up a telephone hidden in a hollow log. The alarm bell awakens the frontier post. To your weapons! The enemy is violating the border! The border guards are already running through the ravines and forests. They look through their binoculars. The infiltrator is getting closer and closer, deeper and deeper inside the border. Maremukha makes up his mind. He sends his trusty friend Hindu on the track of the enemy. Hindu runs along following the scent. The border guards gallop on their

Here's to Your Health,

horses. Maremukha crawls along on his stomach behind Hindu. The enemy is making his way through the thicket, revolver in hand. What a monstrous face! He probably wants to blow up a bridge across the Volga. Or across the Moscow River. He thinks he's going to succeed. What a fool! Now Hindu reaches the trespasser. He sinks his teeth right into the hand that clutches the revolver. A shot rings out, then a second, a third! Missed! Whew! At last, here's Maremukha!

"Put up your hands!"

The spy, baring his teeth with a snarl, unwillingly throws the revolver onto the snow, or onto the grass, and lifts his hands. The border guards, arriving in the nick of time, surround and tie up the trespasser. Well done!

... Only the war erased the feats of Maremukha and his friends from our memory.

Years passed. And I had no further occasion to see the name of Border Guard Maremukha in print. What had become of him?

Twenty years later, I was working in the editorial office one day, and suddenly the door opened and in walked Hindu. Yes, Hindu! I recognized him immediately. Those powerful paws. That tongue ... Hindu was wearing a broad leather collar, hung all over with gold and silver medals and tokens. A champion among Hindus.

A young, well-built border guard was holding Hindu on a leash. The tunic, green epaulets, green cap. His leather boots squeaked when he walked, and the sun was reflected in his gold buttons. What a handsome fellow!

"Hello, Border Guard Maremukha and trusty friend Hindu!" I said, extending my arms in an embrace. "Welcome!"

"I'm not Maremukha," the border guard said sternly, "I'm Demushkin. Colonel Maremukha will be here

Comrade Shifrin!

soon for an interview, following a Kremlin ceremony awarding him a gold medal as a Hero of the Soviet Union."

And, sure enough, in walked Colonel Maremukha. He had a severe, deeply-wrinkled face, and looked a little embarrassed.

We received him in the office of the editor-in-chief, who gave a speech reminding us of the noble border guard's pre-war combat days.

"And this," said the editor-in-chief, pointing to the dog lying on the floor, and to the young border guard accompanying him, "this is the successor to Border Guard Maremukha. Of course, Hindu died long ago of old age. This is another dog—what's his name . . . ?"

"Blizzard!"

". . . Blizzard, who now carries forward with honor the baton of heroic deeds. Even today our valiant border guards safeguard the frontiers of our country, and they are helped in this task by their trusty friends, pressed into service to apprehend each and every violator of our borders!"

The editor spoke at length and with conviction.

I leaned towards Maremukha and whispered in his ear, "Let's go into my office. I have a nice bottle of cognac stored away."

"Let's go!" he said, coming alive.

While young Demushkin and his dog answered the journalists' questions, Maremukha and I went to my office and poured ourselves a couple of glasses of cognac.

I looked at his face, which expressed patient fatigue, at the work-worn, wrinkled hands, at his faded blue eyes, at the decorations and medal stuck on his ill-fitting tunic. . . .

"Ah, Border Guard Maremukha. You know, you were my favorite hero." He smiled, embarrassed. "But all my life one question has interested me. . . . May I ask?"

111

"Why not? Go ahead."

"You see," I said, pouring another round, "you see . . . There you lie in ambush on the border. . . . Along comes the enemy. . . . You take him. . . . Apprehend him, so to speak. And the son-of-a-bitch knows that this is Border Guard Maremukha. After all, you've caught about four hundred of them. Or more. Or a tiny bit less, I don't remember. Well, what would it cost him—the enemy—to go around you. But no, he crawls right towards you, the idiot, the damned spy, the miserable saboteur. . . . What a bastard!"

He smiled sourly, thought a moment, and said, "So what don't you like?"

"Oh, no, I like everything very much. I just want to imagine—you really caught four hundred?"

"Shrewd, aren't you. . . . Here we are 'imagining' together on your bottle of cognac."

"All the same . . . , it's an interesting question."

"Read about it in the newspaper, it is all written up there."

"Of course, everything's written up there. . . . Really, four hundred?"

"Four hundred. It's the truth."

"Do you know what Mark Twain said about the truth?"

"No. What?"

"He said, 'Truth is the greatest treasure. You must use it sparingly.'"

He lit a cigarette, dragged on it greedily. Holding the cigarette Russian-fashion between his thumb and forefinger with the ember towards the inside of his hand, he muttered, "We've used it too sparingly."

"That's what I was saying. . . ."

We drank another.

He looked at me with interest and asked suddenly, "Would *you* ever sell out?"

"What am I, crazy, or something? Of course, I

Comrade Shifrin!

wouldn't sell out. What is there to sell?" I stammered, pouring again.

"You're full of it—you'd sell out," he said, cracking his knuckles. "But it's all over. You know what times those were, the thirties. . . . We were serving on the southern frontier. There they came up with a name: 'border violators.' He's a trespasser, see. He wants to cross the border. But from which side he crosses—that's really of no importance. It's just forbidden to cross, you see?"

I thought, "My good God! The thirties. . . . A camp, surrounded by barbed wire. Watch towers with sharpshooters. Vicious dogs. Unshaven, emaciated, dirty inmates. They've clustered together and are whispering about something, protecting themselves from the wind with the arms of the quilted jackets they're wearing for the third straight year. Then they start running. They gnaw through the barbed wire and make a run for it. From behind them shots are fired, the dogs bark, the wind knocks them off their feet—but they keep running. They make a passage through the taiga, dropping from hunger, keeping away from people and roads. To the south! That's where the border is, that's where there's hope for salvation. They have the wild animal faces of starving men; they gnaw tree bark and fall again. But some, the strongest or the most skillful, make it to the border. There, on the horizon—freedom! There . . .

"And there at the frontier stands Border Guard Maremukha with his trusty friend Hindu, trained to grab men by the throat and by the right arm. A tattered, patched quilted jacket won't save you from his fearsome, hungry jaws.

"Maremukha alone had four hundred such captives! And nearby, another Maremukha, and he also has four hundred! And a third—the same! And each one—the same! Border violators! From whatever direction these 'violators' come—it makes no difference!"

Here's to Your Health,

We smoked and the embers of our cigarettes illuminated his old, worn-out face.

"And what happened afterwards?"

"Afterwards . . . We got stone soup!" he said. "That's the truth: stone soup. Do you think they fed us any differently *there?*"

"You mean you were *there,* too?"

"I was. We were all there. We knew too much. . . . And you, too—watch out!—will know too much."

"And afterwards?"

"Afterwards they remembered about me. . . . Sent me to school, to train dogs. I've seen as many dogs as I care to in my life. And now, it's as if . . . A colonel, and a hero . . . Time goes by. . . . Pour the last round."

We returned to the office of the editor-in-chief.

He was just summing up the interview.

"Thus," he said, "the award always finds a hero. There's always a place for heroic deeds in our life. And we, today's generation of Soviet people, will follow in the footsteps of our forefathers—of whom Colonel Maremukha is a living representative."

"And his trusty friend, the dog Hindu," I said.

The dog lifted his head and looked at me with a long, attentive gaze.

16

AS YOU RIDE the funicular up Mount Mtatsminda, the city unfolds below you. At first you rise up, as if out of a well, onto the roof of a big house on Rustaveli Prospect. Then, as you ascend, you leave behind the little Georgian pastry shops where in the morning you eat burning hot pastries, holding them smartly by their little dough navels. The next thing to drop away is Hotel Sakartvelo, from whose windows you looked sleepily at the red-brick walls of the maternity hospital, with its squeals of newborn infants. Then the Kura River, which rushes breathlessly past the old city with its amphitheater of picturesque dead-ends and narrow streets: too narrow for two cars to pass one another, or even two pedestrians, especially if both are coming home from intimate little parties where more than one toast was raised to "flourishing Georgia and the wonderful guests she has the honor to welcome." And then you have the whole city in the palm of your hand, all airy and pink from the innumerable tiled roofs. It reminds you either of Paris or of Prague, where you have never once been, or of some unusually beautiful imaginary place, the search for which was the very thing that led you to this marvelous city—Tbilisi!

Here's to Your Health,

The tiny cable car carries you higher and higher, to the mountain heights. The polite, moustachioed conductor opens the door and you're—free! Perhaps no other word will do. You breathe freely, filling your lungs with the sweet Georgian air, and look long and admiringly, as if through smoke-colored glasses, at the pink Tbilisi paradise, and the foothills somewhere far beyond the city, and the steppe, where you imagine you can see the curve of the earth. Mtatsminda was the culmination of our trip.

Before that, we spent two days rushing around in an old, dilapidated Molotov, driving along the Kakhetian roads, reading with delight the names of the settlements which sprang up with each turn: Tsinandali, Mukuzani, Gurdzhaani—places which give their names to fine Georgian wines.

"When we get back to Tbilisi, I'll make you *satsivi* chicken."

"Yes!" said Otar. "She makes divine *satsivi*. Stop the jalopy! We'll buy some chickens."

Otar was a poet, and made up his mind about things quickly. In front of us stood a bazaar, where slender old women dressed in black traded in everything one would need to feed and toast a guest.

I loved bazaars. I loved to wander among the rows of stalls filled with tomatoes, shiny washed apples, sacks of sunflower seeds, and milkcans full of sour cream. Shouting tradesmen juggled watermelons, stabbing them with terrifying knives to make the sweet watermelon juice flow out like blood. I loved to watch them grunt, plunge their knives into the green watermelon, and pull out crisp, triangular plugs for buyers to inspect. I loved to haggle with the women, offering them a third of what they asked. They would shout, threaten, curse rapturously, invite me to "sample the product," and

Comrade Shifrin!

finally back down, sighing and grumbling. Their eyes, however, betrayed respect for the serious customer.

I had loved the romance of the bazaar ever since the time I had swaggered around the marketplace of a small Crimean resort town, trying to hide my hunger. I was a skinny, unshaven, sunburned student then, wearing an outlandish, torn red pajama top, a red bandana around my neck. I stopped by the sour cream vendor and, looking with concentration at the sky, plunged my finger into a pitcher to "test" whether it was sour. The woman stared at me in amazement, and I asked, "How much?" She gave her answer. "What?!" I shouted with mock horror, and walked to the next vendor, holding out my "testing" finger.

"How much?" I yelled to the old woman with the sunflower seeds, greedily cracking the sample I had grabbed from her sack.

"How much?" I asked the apple vendor, crunching into his saffron goods.

"How much?" I bullied the watermelon woman, fat and jolly, looking as though she'd hidden a watermelon in her blouse and another under her skirt.

"That one's fifty kopecks!" she laughed, showing her teeth.

"You're out of your mind!" I shrieked, drooling at the sight of the crimson melon, covered with wasps. "Fifteen."

"Drop dead, beggar!" she yelled. "Forty-five!"

"What did we fight the Revolution for?" I roared, gathering a crowd. "Twenty!"

"Whatever we fought for, we're stuck with it!" she snarled. "Thirty-five, or get lost!"

"This is unheard of!" I fussed. "Thirty-five kopecks for this cucumber?! That's robbery, Madame!"

Here's to Your Health,

"Go to hell!" she exploded. "I ain't no 'Madame'; we don't have no more fancy madames! Thirty! And that's final!"

"What's your real price?" I said angrily, as if I were losing my patience.

"You got no money anyway, college boy!" she laughed. "Go on, take it, you damned skeleton!" and she tossed me a warm, heavy watermelon with an uneven crack, smelling of honey, sugar, and God knows what else. I climbed onto an empty counter, sat down Tatar-style, my legs crossed under me, and—crack!—broke the watermelon into two uneven halves.

I picked up the smaller half like a bowl and sank my hungry-student's teeth into the jagged, pink flesh. My eyes closed with pleasure, the sweet juice ran down my bare chest, the wind ruffled my red pajama top. *That was bliss!*

Reliving old times, I prepared to help Otar buy a chicken at this Georgian bazaar.

"How much?" I asked.

"Ten," said the vendor.

She looked at me calmly and derisively. Her chickens were calm and derisive, too.

"Seven," I mumbled uncertainly.

"Ten," she said, turning away. The chickens turned away, too.

"Otar, ten," I said. I had evidently lost my touch.

Otar grabbed the chickens by the legs and tossed them into the trunk. The chickens complained, offended, and then settled themselves with dignity on the warm, gasoline-smelling rags.

We continued along past vineyards and green lakes, over ravines, around mountains, looping with the road and singing, "You stand on the other shore . . ." in three-part harmony.

I have always been surprised at how politely the

Comrade Shifrin!

Georgians listen to us singing their songs. They manage to keep a straight face as we cheerfully murder their wonderful songs, singing painfully out of tune and missing the beat. Although we usually sing in unison, for some reason we let loose in Georgia and allow ourselves to sing in parts. God, how we try!

Otar listened, Maria even joined in, and we overcame our embarrassment and drawled out, "You stand on the other shore . . ." Luckily, I didn't know all the words, and so had to shut up in disgrace. And then—oh, that Georgian tact!—Maria started to sing softly. She had a low, muffled voice which got into your soul, and oh, those marvelous, always unexpected throaty sounds born of the collision of two or three consonants. The song rose up from the road, straightened out, and then —miracle of miracles—flew ahead of us. "You stand on the other shore . . ." Even Otar came to life, somehow unnoticed, and very softly added his baritone to the fabric of the melody. "You stand on the other shore . . ."

They both looked at the road and sang. And if a hitchhiker had appeared ahead of our car at that moment, he, too, would have begun to sing so well and so musically that one would have thought the three of them had sung together all their lives. It seemed that every tree and roadside bush moved in time to the music, "You stand on the other shore . . ." Recovered from my embarrassment, I, too, sang along softly, so as not to interfere with the song. This bliss had no bounds. The song was as invigorating as the fresh Georgian air. "You stand on the other shore . . ."

"Otar, I want to eat!" Maria said suddenly. Oh, that Maria! Millions of men in Russia dream of such a woman. Against the background of general emancipation, Maria was a miracle. She had seen, or, rather, felt, that I was listening hungrily, mouth watering, to the weak cackle coming from the trunk. Oh, that Maria

Here's to Your Health,

... While the men were talking about poetry, soccer, politics, she gazed mysteriously out the window, listening now to us, now to herself.

"What do you think, Maria?"

"It's hard to say right away. There could be several opinions here. Don't you want some wine?"

The car turned off onto an asphalt road which led into the woods. The forest ended abruptly and—I'd never get used to these Georgian miracles—we found ourselves in front of a snow-white building. A forest tavern, or, rather, a restaurant, for such chance travelers as ourselves.

Six men, majestic and silent, were sitting at a long wooden table. Behind them, a group of musicians. The table was covered with pitchers of wine, which were refilled from huge vats set into the floor. At just the right moment the bartender would ladle more wine into the empty pitchers.

The six were having some sort of celebration. They sat with their glasses raised like the princes in Pirosmani's painting. Politely uttering the usual greeting, "*Gamardzhoba,*" we sat down quietly at a far table, ordered shashlyk, and relaxed. One of the six made a sign with his handkerchief, and the musicians began to strike their drums.

One of the men, older than the rest, stood up and threw one arm behind his head. He instantly became slenderer and taller, his face lit up with joy, and slowly he turned a circle in front of the table. All of a sudden, he stooped down, cried out, and, straightening up like a shot, stepped backwards with tiny steps. He raised his eyebrows, signalling an invitation to the next man. This one, somewhat younger, jumped out into the middle of the room like a cat, and ta-ta-ta-ta-ta-ta! danced like a ballerina on point the length of the table. He held a skewer in one hand. The musicians beat out the melody faster and more rhythmically. Ah! The skewer pierced

Comrade Shifrin!

the log ceiling. Then a third, and a fourth, began to dance like the heroes on the coins of Ochauri. It seemed they were wearing not white nylon shirts and fashionable slacks, but Circassian battle coats; waving not skewers, but steel daggers. The heroes were locked now in mortal combat, and ravens would soon tear at their young, still warm bodies, taut as bowstrings. Ah! The skewers stabbed the ceiling! The music shrilled ever wilder, becoming more and more primitive. Their legs, sinewy and slender, moved ever faster over the floor boards, until it seemed they could go no faster. Any minute now they would drop from exhaustion. But still the music mounted and the excitement increased. . . . Ho! Everything ended on some incredibly high note, beyond even the range of Yma Sumac. The dancers sat down at the table to drink their wine—to thin their surging blood, cool their flushed heads. . . .

"You know," said Otar, "this evening you must go with me to see Batono Lado. What a man! A great man . . ."

While we drove through the city, Otar told me that, as far as he was concerned, there were five painters in Georgia who could equal the glory of all the painters of Western Europe. They were Piromanishvili, Kakabadze, Kikodze, Akhvlediani, and Gudiashvili. Batono Lado, whom we were on our way to visit, was Lado Gudiashvili, the patriarch of Georgian art. His hospitality and wisdom were nearly the biggest tourist attractions of Tbilisi.

That evening, freshly pressed and wearing ties, we knocked at the door of a two-story house on a quiet little street. The door was opened for us by a woman of regal bearing, Nina Alexandrovna Gudiashvili.

"Lado is expecting you."

We ascended a long, dark staircase to the second story and found ourselves in a museum. Hundreds of canvases covered the walls of the enormous hall. Near the door was a gray-haired man with a noble, clean-shaven face. He had ironic, kind (I thought) blue eyes. In Georgia, it is customary to call great people by their first names. No patronymic is needed, or surname, and everyone knows who you mean.

"Do you remember how Titsian . . . ?"
"Paolo's book came out in Leningrad. . . ."
"Iraklii will speak at the Congress. . . ."
"You haven't been to see Lado yet?! Go right away. . . ."

This is not familiarity, it's the greatest respect. And it's not necessary to explain that Titsian is Tabidze, Paolo is Yashvili, Iraklii is Abashidze. . . .

I heard only one person referred to constantly by name and patronymic, though never by surname: Boris Leonidovich (Pasternak).

"Boris Leonidovich sat on this chair. . . ."
"Boris Leonidovich, translating my poems . . ."
"Boris Leonidovich loved to stay with us. . . ."
"Boris Leonidovich would say to me that it's best to drink Armenian cognac in just these glasses," Batono Lado said in a soft voice, going around to each of us at the table and pouring cognac into small, gold tumblers. We were completely overwhelmed by all we had seen, and timidly murmured, "For goodness' sake, Lado. Let us do it ourselves, let us pour for you."

"Don't deny Lado this small pleasure," his wife said gently, her eyes wrinkling in a smile. "Lado loves guests."

She spoke about Lado in the third person.
"Lado painted this picture in Paris. . . ."
"Lado dedicated this picture to the memory of Pirosmani. . . ."

And he stood right there, short and slender, embarrassed by our visit, which took him away from his work: on the easel stood the portrait of the blue woman.

Comrade Shifrin!

In his works it was possible to study a half century of painting. Here were all the great currents of twentieth century art cleverly and complexly interwoven: the inspiration and enthusiasm of the twenties, the tragedy of the thirties, the hopes of the forties, the searches of the fifties, and the discoveries of the sixties. And behind all this richness, turmoil, and reflection, stood the solid and unique mark of Lado Gudiashvili, a man who could express the spirit of his people.

As we said good-bye, vying with each other to voice our gratitude, we assured him that his works would surely soon be acclaimed at galleries in Moscow and abroad. He repeated wryly, "God grant it, God grant it." Then suddenly he beamed like a child and said, "My young friends! Is that the important thing? Every man has his pleasure—mine is to finish this portrait."

The blue woman gazed at us invitingly and sadly.

"Good-bye, Batono Lado! May you live a thousand years, Batono Lado!"

For a long time he waved to us from the balcony, and the night lantern illuminated his small, slender figure, throwing an enormous shadow onto the front of his two-story sanctuary.

We went out onto an empty Rustaveli Prospect. It was three in the morning. Single passersby looked at us with surprise. We were thrilled, moved, enlightened by our contact with art, and we chattered loudly about some nonsense, about something of absolutely no consequence, carrying away in our souls the important thing, the main thing: the words, gestures, colors, and smells of the wondrous house we had just left.

She was walking alone, carrying a string bag which held an aluminum pot. She could have walked right out of a canvas by the unforgettable Pirosmani—wearing a shapeless white blouse and a short, black skirt which cut into her fleshy, fat legs. She was big and dark, simultaneously thirty and forty-five. A jolly gold tooth shone in her provocative mouth. She was singing. The few male passersby flew at her like hawks, but she walked on, ignoring them, and the men froze behind her, immobile as the trees on Rustaveli Prospect.

"My God," I groaned, "what is this? Hold me back, my friends, or I won't be responsible for my actions."

When she passed by, I knelt down and offered her a flower.

"Don't fool around!" Otar whispered to me. "That's Marika, Tbilisi's prostitute. Our only one."

"Good evening, Marika," I said. "We're reading poetry, come walk with us along this glorious street, lit weakly by the moon."

She stood before me, examining me and pondering. Then she walked towards me, took me by the hand like a child, and crooned, "Do you know this poem?"

> The silent steppe turns blue,
> The peaks of the Caucasus ring it 'round;
> Above the sea they frown and calmly doze,
> Like giants bending over some great shield . . .

We just stood there, astonished and speechless. And this miracle, Marika, smiled with her gold tooth and said, "Lermontov. Mikhail."

She walked on, crooning her unintelligible song. But I caught up with her and said, "Marika, we'll drive you home."

"Ah, what a nice boy," she said. "Drive me." And she grinned like a satyr, winking her black, gypsy eye. We grabbed a taxi and started for the new section of town in which she lived. But we hadn't gone a hundred meters before, all of a sudden—ta-da!—like lightning, a blue Volga with a red stripe whizzed by and stopped, blocking our way.

Comrade Shifrin!

"Ay," said Marika wearily, and somehow very simply. "They're after me. . . ." She pressed herself into the seat, suddenly becoming small and old.

A sergeant with round, apathetic eyes got out of the police car, sat down next to our driver, and ordered him to drive off somewhere to the right. We turned right again, and then left. The blue Volga with the red stripe followed us. They brought us to a building smelling of fresh paint. A handsome fellow with graying temples, black moustache, and blue eyes stood up from behind a table and said cheerfully, "Judging from your embarrassed faces, you're Muscovites. In the name of the Tbilisi police I welcome you to our city, and I congratulate you that my colleagues, vigilantly protecting the morality of Tbilisi residents and their guests, have saved you much unpleasantness—and, speaking man to man, you will understand me very well."

"Excuse me," I said, "we were driving along the street and we saw this housewife alone, going home to the bosom of her family. Any scholar and gentleman would have driven her home, especially as it was on our way. We demand that you release this woman immediately and save her from *this* unpleasantness, which she does not deserve. Speaking man to man, you will understand me very well!"

"Listen to this, Marika!" exclaimed the handsome supervisor. "Go on home, and no nonsense!"

He turned to us. "And which hotel are the respected guests of the capital of our republic staying in?" We told him.

"Givi," he addressed the round-faced sergeant, "see the comrades to their hotel. We wish you good health—which you still enjoy thanks to the Tbilisi police—and great creative achievements!"

We exchanged bows, and an enormous Black Maria took us back to the Sakartvelo. An awakening Tbilisi

Here's to Your Health,

was dimly perceptible through the car's mesh-covered windows.

. . . If you look down at Tbilisi from Mtatsminda, below the mosaic of tiled roofs you can make out small, green courtyards in which children play, always well-dressed and beautiful. Narrow, winding streets flow like rivulets into the broad, straight avenues where groups of young men stroll unhurriedly, not paying the least attention to passing women. Suddenly, a colorfully-dressed Kurdish woman flashes by. An old man in a black cap and soft slippers slowly lights up his short pipe. Street lights go on in long, thin garlands, giving the city a festive, New Year's look. The gray evening fog covers the mountains in the east. In the west a narrow, orange band still limns the horizon.

17

HAVE YOU SEEN the Moscow "drop-inns"? These are booths scattered here and there around the side streets. From time to time they change their "Beer" sign to "Cider." Most often, though, you'll see a sign saying "Out of Beer." At those times, the bored vendor, a fat, rude Katka or Maruska, will eat a sandwich with gusto, smacking her lips and insulting passersby. She's become rich by selling a lot of foam and a little beer, poured into badly washed pint mugs ("half-a-glass," as the old-timers and policemen affectionately call this transparent operation).

At the end of the day, working people stand in ever-lengthening lines in order to treat themselves to a mug of draft beer. The line moves slowly, as each person takes two, and maybe even three, mugs. The fellow who discovers a hunk of salted fish stashed away in his pocket becomes a prince, a god. He ritually divides the fish just so, licks each bone clean, sucks it, and even gives a little piece to his neighbor in line. On another part of the line, a conversation trickles on. Someone tells a joke about the Civil War hero Chapayev; and about some woman, a real decent woman, a first-class woman, who was a real hit the night before at the

Here's to Your Health,

dances at Ostankino, made it with everyone, God bless her, what a broad; and about the government, must be we've had it up to here with the government, although, you bet your life, they've got their problems, too. . . .

The "drop-inn" is a beer stand, club, snack bar, and place to relax where after work you can split a bottle of vodka three ways, or maybe even two ways. You keep this bottle hidden in that inside pocket of your jacket reserved for the "very special goods" bought as a joint undertaking and wrapped in a newspaper so the police don't see. You stand around in a tight circle, pour a little beer in for color, and live it up!

Of course, there are no tables in these booths, so people make themselves comfortable as best they can. Someone sits on the garbage can spread with newspaper, someone else on a pile of bricks, and others just stand around in groups. And they drink their beer. This standing arrangement is planned purposely so that people don't gather, don't chatter about forbidden topics. Just drink up your mugful and go home, to your wife, to your kids, to your television set.

The men disperse unwillingly, even though they don't have much money to spend.

"Vaska, lend me a ruble until payday."

"Come on, I don't even have it for myself."

"I'll give it back on the twentieth. I'm getting a bonus."

"What do you think I am, some greedy Yid? When I say no, I mean no."

I loved the beer stand on my street. That is, I loved to watch the people drink. Sometimes I stood in line myself. You could drink your beer, listen to what was being said around you—rub up against life. Otherwise, as Lenin said of Herzen, your horizons are painfully narrow, you're terribly far removed from the people. . . .

There was one old guy whom I had been seeing in the

Comrade Shifrin!

line for some time. He was always hanging around uncertainly, letting people cut in front of him. He was shabbily dressed, very clean, somehow unsure of himself. In short, not really one of us. His gaze met mine, something in him trembled, and he said to the person standing behind him, "Pardon me, I'm going away for a second. I was standing here, I'll be right back...." His "pardon me" jarred me somehow. It was out of place here. After all, he wasn't in a restaurant. When you're drinking beer at Katka's, who needs "pardon me"? No, he wasn't one of us.

He walked up to me and said, "You're not by any chance a collector?"

"Well, sort of—no. What have you got?"

"You see, I'm a little short of money, maybe you'd buy . . . ?"

He opened his hand, revealing a medal "For Combat Services." I was a bit startled.

"Well, okay," I said. "What's it worth? How much do you need?"

"Oh, fifty kopecks, perhaps."

I gave him a half-ruble, and he ran to his place on line.

Later we found ourselves side by side and were slowly drinking our beer. Suddenly he began to tell me about himself, just like that. He spoke in such a refined Moscow accent that it stuck in my memory. I'll try to convey it, retaining even the intonation, with only a little bit of my own, just a hint, the littlest bit. . . .

The little railroad station was desolate. It looked black against the white snow like a charred firebrand, and only the white strips of tape crisscrossing the windows gave it a kind of incongruously festive look. "My God, are they really bombing here, too. . . ." Vladimir Nikolaevich exclaimed in horror. He clutched to his chest a worn-out, very unmilitary suitcase filled with presents: a piece of soap, a bit of tallow, thick American chocolate, and camel's hair socks.

The train on which Vladimir Nikolaevich had arrived had already pulled away. Actually, it had never really come to a stop—it just slowed down. A woman conductor in a quilted jacket and iron-rimmed glasses had said sternly, "Looks like your stop . . . ," and Vladimir Nikolaevich had jumped down heavily into the soft, crunching snow. The train whistled piercingly, like a rabbit, picked up speed, and went on somewhere beyond the Urals, maybe to Novosibirsk.

Vladimir Nikolaevich made his way through a crowd of women carrying bundles and crying children. They were as shabby and neglected as this Ural station, and smelled of some peculiar, acrid, railroad station smell.

"Comrade soldier, may I see your papers!"

Vladimir Nikolaevich stuck his hand into his inside pocket for his leave pass. He had become accustomed to this peremptory challenge. At each station the patrols checked the papers of military men coming from the west.

"You're here on what business?" a weary, unshaven captain asked sternly.

"Personal business. To see my wife and bring her this food. And my daughter. They've been evacuated here. . . ."

"You may proceed," said the captain. "Don't forget to check in at the commandant's office. You have three days left."

"Yes sir, Comrade Captain."

All the municipal government bureaus were located on the railroad station square. A long, two-story building was hung with makeshift signs announcing: District Committee, District Executive Committee, Police, Post Office, Military Induction Center.

Vladimir Nikolaevich thought a moment and went into the induction center.

Comrade Shifrin!

"What is it you want?"
"How can I get to the village called Malye Kotly?"
"It's about fifteen kilometers from here. . . ."
"Is there some kind of car?"
"Are you joking? A car . . . But try at the post office. They take the mail out there in a horsecart. Ask them, maybe they'll give you a lift. . . . Otherwise, just tuck your feet under your arms and start marching. . . ."

At the post office, a woman in a sheepskin was loading the horsecart. Vladimir Nikolaevich approached her.

"Uh, excuse me, citizen. Please, I beg of you. I haven't seen my wife in three years. And my daughter is now three years old. Can you help me get to Malye Kotly?"

"I'm telling you, dearie, this horse won't get the two of us there! Look what shape she's in—skin and bones. She tries to pull the two of us, she'll drop dead. Anyway, she belongs to the government. They could arrest me . . ."

"My dear citizen, please, listen, I've been traveling for six days. It'll take me all night to get there. I just can't . . . I'll give you some soap. A brand new piece. I swear, brand new . . ."

Vladimir Nikolaevich hurriedly opened his little suitcase, took out the piece of soap, and offered it to the woman in the sheepskin.

She took the soap, weighed it in her palm, and looked with chagrin at the horse.

"She won't make it, the bitch. Sure thing, she'll just drop along the road. . . . I'll carry your suitcase . . . and you walk alongside. That's better."

"Oh, thank you, oh, that's fine," murmured Vladimir Nikolaevich, arranging his suitcase on the cart.

"Look out you don't fall behind," said the woman, waving her whip. "Ho! Come on, you damned nag!"

Vladimir Nikolaevich waved his arms and slapped them against his sides—cold!—rubbed his ears and

131

walked along behind the stumpy, emaciated horse.
   At first he tried to sing something to himself in time with his steps:

>   Morning paints with tender color
>   On the Kremlin's ancient walls. . . .

He knew that he couldn't carry a tune, so he didn't sing aloud, but just hummed the melody in time with the horse's gait. It worked out well. He remembered the May Day celebration. . . .

>   Morning paints with tender color
>   On the Kremlin's ancient walls. . . .

   . . . The song started somewhere around the Sretensky Gate. Everyone was marching in columns, smartly dressed in white shirts and wide, pressed, denim trousers. Nina was walking beside him, her small, rough hand clasped in his. She was wearing a long, flowered dress with a red bow fastened at her breast.

>   Powerful, invincible . . .

A brass band blared up ahead, and walking was so pleasant on this light, sunny day. Especially with Nina by his side. From time to time she would turn her head and look up at him, and he would blush and turn away shyly, feeling tall and clumsy.

>   Higher, higher, higher
>   Fly our metal birds of war;
>   "Protect the workers' homeland,"
>   Their mighty engines roar . . .

Comrade Shifrin!
"Long live great Stalin!"
"Hoorah!"
"Glory to great Stalin!"
"Hoorah!!!"
"Hoorah!" he shouted, waving paper roses, and Nina jokingly put her hands over her ears, and looked up at him with fright, just like this . . .

. . . The horse had been walking for some time. She was no longer dragging, but trotted easily along the snowy, windswept road.
Vladimir Nikolaevich did not lag behind. He also trotted.

How fine to gallop on the steppe,
How fine to breathe its clean free air . . .

. . . Those Americans were really funny. Allies . . . And their songs were funny. Volodka Lebeshev picked them up somewhere and brought them into the company. When there was no political commissar around, everyone would sing their favorite Volodka-tune, in harmony, "There's a tavern in the town . . ." And everyone would yell, "In the town . . . !"
". . . And there my true love sits her down . . ." And Vladimir Nikolaevich also yelled, "Sits her down!" Volodka Lebeshev frowned at this off-key contribution, but didn't say anything—he was a kind fellow. He would most likely become an actor after the war.

. . . "Huh! Now she's started running, damned horse," grumbled the woman in the sheepskin. "She would get it into her head at just the wrong time. Some kind of Hitler, not a horse—she should go to hell!"
Vladimir Nikolaevich also quickened his step. How surprised Nina would be! He would creep silently up to

Here's to Your Health,

the hut. Tap, tap . . . Who's there? Excuse me, do Nina and Natasha Polyakov live here?

Vladimir Nikolaevich began to laugh softly, covering his mouth with his hand. Silly, of course, but very nice. . . .

 . . . He had really wiped the nose of that lanky engineer who was courting Nina. . . .

When he started working at the factory after technical school, he immediately took a liking to that girl. She was stern and beautiful. Vladimir Nikolaevich told his relief, Vitka Morozov, "You see that girl? I'd marry her tomorrow."

And Vitka Morozov had said, "And do you see that lanky engineer? He'll show you such a tomorrow, you won't see the day after tomorrow."

After the change of shift the next day, Vladimir Nikolaevich ran to the gate to lie in wait for the girl. There she was. Vladimir Nikolaevich felt a knot in his chest; his mouth went dry. He couldn't inhale or exhale. He walked up to the girl and said in a strange, unpleasant voice, "Why don't we go to the movies this evening?"

The girl looked attentively at the blushing Vladimir Nikolaevich and replied, "In principle, I am against casual flirtations, comrade foreman."

"My God! What flirtations, why casual flirtations?" flew into Vladimir Nikolaevich's head. "What is she talking about? I meant something entirely different. How could she think that?" But out loud he said, "Well, that's a shame. I simply wanted . . ."

"So much the worse," said the girl, walking on.

"Blockhead, cretin, idiot!" Vladimir Nikolaevich chastised himself. Everything had slipped through his fingers.

Nina had only to pass by accidentally, and he would stop work, stunned, and gaze after her. . . . The women

134

Comrade Shifrin!

in the shop whispered among themselves and giggled, but Vladimir Nikolaevich felt depressed and dull. He would lower his eyes, sigh, and go back to his work.

Once at the club they showed a new movie called *Mashenka*. Vladimir Nikolaevich spotted Nina as he entered the hall. She was sitting alone. The film had not yet begun. Like a blind man, he made his way towards her down the row, stepping on people's toes. "Pardon, excuse me, pardon." He sat down next to her. It was someone else's seat. Some fat fellow was already coming towards them. Vladimir Nikolaevich mustered all his strength and looked so plaintively at the fat man that the latter started, glanced at Nina, and went off to find another seat. Vladimir Nikolaevich did not move a muscle throughout the whole movie. He felt Nina breathing next to him. From time to time he forgot himself—the movie was excellent—but then he would return again with joy to the thought that he was sitting next to Nina. He even laughed softly, and Nina looked at him sternly. Afraid that she would get angry, he covered his mouth with his hand so as not to laugh and begged forgiveness with a pleading look.

When the movie had ended and everyone had left the hall, Vladimir Nikolaevich said, "How marvelous, what a wonderful film. May I see you home, Nina?"

Nina laughed wryly. "I still have half an hour. You can walk me to Suvorov Boulevard, if you want to. I'm going to meet someone there."

Vladimir Nikolaevich was so embarrassed, so mortified, that he could just, could just . . . Oh, how could anyone make fun of a person that way? I should deliver her to a date . . . ? Excuse me . . . There's a limit to everything. I also have my pride.

"All right," he said, turning pale and pressing his lips together. "I'll walk you to your appointment."

They walked along Suvorov Boulevard, and he talked, talked, talked. . . . And she smiled and interjected her comments, clever and funny. And he talked and talked and talked.

"Well," she said, "here we are. Thank you for walking me here."

The lanky engineer got up from a bench, shaking his head reproachfully and tapping his finger against the face of his watch.

"Good-bye," said Nina, walking off with her engineer.

"Nina," Vladimir Nikolaevich called suddenly, "you won't forget that we have our wedding in five days?" And he turned and walked off in the other direction. The engineer's jaw dropped. He looked after Vladimir Nikolaevich, stunned. It must have been funny, because Nina started laughing.

"Engineers," Vladimir Nikolaevich thought maliciously. "What did she see in those engineers? Just think, engineers..."

..."Well, are you tired?" asked the woman in the sheepskin. "My, my, how you're walking. Sit down here, it's all right. I'll get down if I have to."

"No, no, don't worry," said Vladimir Nikolaevich, "I've sort of gotten used to it. Do we have far to go?"

"No, not too far, about eight miles. Why don't you get on. For God's sake, climb in. I feel guilty somehow. And the mare is kind of clopping along, she'll make it somehow. Climb in, will you? Climb in, soldier-boy...."

"No, it's all right. Do you take the mail every day?"

"Every day?! Are you kidding? Twice a week. The women wait. Letters, parcels, death notices.... They're starving, see... Can't get along without menfolk...."

...Vladimir Nikolaevich could not hold out. On the second day he went to the personnel office, got Nina's address, and wrote her a letter. "Nina, Nina, Nina

Comrade Shifrin!
... Call me. I need you very, very much...." Two days later she called.
"You wrote to me, you can't deny it," she said.
"I won't deny it," said Vladimir Nikolaevich, shuddering. On June twentieth they registered their marriage. On June twenty-fourth Vladimir Nikolaevich arrived at the induction center.

"Company, attention!"
"Red Army comrades . . . Our special detachment will defend Moscow to the last drop of blood. Our troops are now defending the approaches to the capital of our homeland. It's our job to make every home a fortress in case the Germans break through to Moscow."
Vladimir Nikolaevich's platoon was assigned a house on Pervaya Meshchanskaya Street. It very conveniently had three exposures, controlling Sretenka, Kolkhoz Square, and Grokholskii Alley.
"Will it really come to this?" Vladimir Nikolaevich whispered to Volodka Lebeshev. "The Krauts in Moscow? They've got to be crazy. . . ."
"We are sure that the Red Army will stop the enemy at the gates of Moscow, but the NKVD troops must be ready for anything. To your barracks!"

... A village appeared ahead of them.
"Is that ours?" Vladimir Nikolaevich asked hopefully.
"No, that's only Gorokhovka," said the woman in the sheepskin. "We still have a way to trudge, God help us! Climb into the cart, I say. . . ."
Women poured out of the houses, hurriedly tying their scarves on their heads. They stood on the porches and near the fences and stared tensely at Vladimir Nikolaevich: whose man is coming? They looked si-

lently from under their hands and did not avert their eyes when Vladimir Nikolaevich said softly and uncertainly, "Hello . . ."

They were all different, these women—some were young and others old, some came from the city and some from the country; a few in gray shawls and others wearing white, fluffy hats, in felt boots or light summer shoes, wearing quilted jackets or with autumn coats thrown over their shoulders. Some were comforting children. And all of them stared silently at Vladimir Nikolaevich's back as he walked awkwardly behind the cart in his long, shapeless overcoat and canvas boots.

"Hello," he said softly, "Hello . . ."

. . . "Hello, comrades," said Captain Shuleko, entering the barracks. "Here are some rookies for us. Please welcome them and make them feel at home. Whoever mistreats them—I'll have his head! They'll wear civilian clothes for the time being."

The "rookies" were rough-looking and no longer young.

Captain Shuleko himself looked after them. He chased them around the parade ground, taught them the drills, and affectionately called them "motherfuckers." The rookies weren't offended. They lived separately, and when the soldiers approached them, they became silent.

"Well, how is it, fellows, hard on you?" Volodka Lebeshev would ask.

"Not too bad, we'll live," the rookies would say.

One night there was a combat alert. The division was loaded into heated freight cars and taken to the Caucasus. There were no stops. Other trains obediently yielded the right of way.

" 'The tired sun tenderly parted from the sea,' " recited Volodka Lebeshev. He had never been to the sea and was dreaming about going swimming.

Comrade Shifrin!

"You know," he said to Vladimir Nikolaevich, "all my life I've dreamed of going to the Black Sea. I even saved money—in August I was supposed to get a vacation—but, no! Hitler got in the way, the bastard. Well, I thought, I'll go after the war. See how lucky it turned out, the war's not even over and I'm already going to the sea. Not so bad after all. Maybe I'll even drop in on Paris, take a look at how the French proletariat lives. . . ."

Tout va très bien,
Madame la Marquise . . .

The train stopped on the steppe. The soldiers were lined up and their orders were read to them:

"For treason against the Homeland and complicity with the enemy, the inhabitants of this region will be resettled in other areas of the country. . . . The operation must be carried out in two hours. . . . Authorized officers will be in charge."

Then the rookies got off the train. Some rookies! Lieutenant colonels, majors, captains.

"What do you think of that!" Volodka Lebeshev exclaimed excitedly. "A real conspiracy, just like in the movies."

Vladimir Nikolaevich's platoon approached an obscure little village clinging to the foothills. A lieutenant colonel, one of the "rookies," gave the final instructions: the soldiers were to enter the houses, read the orders, and give the inhabitants two hours to pack their most valuable possessions to take with them. In two hours all the inhabitants must be loaded into the railroad cars which would carry them to their destinations.

Vladimir Nikolaevich, Volodka Lebeshev, and two other soldiers knocked at the last house on the street. No one answered the door. The soldiers knocked louder. An aged voice behind the door asked something, not in Russian.

"Open up, open up, Mother, we're on your side!" shouted Volodka Lebeshev.

There was whispering behind the door, then the bolts began to rumble. A little old woman peeked out with fright from behind the door, and, catching sight of soldiers with automatic weapons, yelled something into the room.

Vladimir Nikolaevich entered. The soldiers lit lanterns, illuminating the plain, clay walls, tiny blind window, and clay floor. An old man stood in his underwear, and behind him hid the old woman and two children who stared with sleepy black eyes.

"Can they speak Russian?" asked Volodka, growing timid.

"We can, we can," the old man said in a muffled voice.

Vladimir Nikolaevich took out the order and read it apologetically.

"It will be nice there," he unexpectedly added on his own. "Please, don't worry."

He looked at the old woman and was seized with unbearable pity. Where would she go from this clay-walled hut of hers? He expected tears, shouts, entreaties. . . .

"Do you mean just me and the old woman, or all of us?" asked the old man.

"All of you," said Volodka Lebeshev reassuringly. "Don't worry, Pop, it's the same for everyone. This order came. . . ."

The soldiers went out onto the porch, lit cigarettes, inhaled.

"God damn it," said Volodka. "If that were my mother. . . ."

"Don't chatter!" a soldier with a lantern said sullenly. "They're traitors, didn't you hear?"

Comrade Shifrin!

"Yeah, I heard." Volodka, too, was sullen.
Two hours later the inhabitants of the village were moving slowly along the road. The soldiers stood on either side and watched them drag sacks with their belongings—some phonographs, boards, rags, slaughtered rams, bawling children, mirrors. A man in glasses was carrying a globe. On the steppe freight cars stretched as far as the eye could see. From all directions across the steppe, on the roads and on the grass, people walked, some with bundles and others without. And there, too, were the old man and the old woman; the children hung on to her skirt. They marched silently past Vladimir Nikolaevich.
"Good-bye," he said softly.
"Good-bye," said the old man, smiling bitterly. . . .
"Well done!" said the "rookie" lieutenant colonel. "The operation went smoothly. Each soldier will be given ten days' leave."

"Let me get off," said the woman in the sheepskin.
"Ugh, this damned nag, she's begun to limp, may she croak. But you stay put, stay where you are, I say. The nag belongs to the government, but your legs don't. Huh, he's off somewhere. Maybe you're sleeping?"
"No, I'm not sleeping. Just . . ."
Vladimir Nikolaevich was very tired; his legs were frozen and were beginning to feel like wood. It had grown completely dark.
The village loomed up suddenly from around a turn. Vladimir Nikolaevich was taken aback.
"So," nodded the woman in the sheepskin. "Here's Kotly. You made it, soldier-boy."
The cart creaked unbearably through the snow, through the darkness, as if someone were scraping a giant fork across a plate. The huts blackened indistinctly against the gray clouds. There was not a light nor a person to be seen.

"Where should I go?" wondered Vladimir Nikolaevich. His steps crunched evenly after the cart. The rusty creaking tore through the silence of the village. It seemed to Vladimir Nikolaevich that everyone would be awakened. He even walked several paces on tiptoes.

"Which hut?" asked the woman.

"I don't know exactly. Nina wrote me that it was Vasilisa's hut."

"Which Vasilisa? Tikhova, maybe?"

"I don't know, to tell the truth . . ."

"Well, let's go, we'll call someone."

The horse came to a halt, and the woman climbed down from the cart with a grunt and walked over to the nearest house. Dogs started barking, first yapping uncertainly, then louder and louder and more viciously. . . .

Vladimir Nikolaevich recalled that there, in the Caucasus, dogs were also barking . . . yelping and whining. Dogs barked the same way everywhere.

The woman knocked on the door with her whip, and when someone looked out the window, she started whispering in the dark.

Vladimir Nikolaevich suddenly realized that he would be seeing Nina and Natashka that very minute; in an instant he would be returned to that long-ago time before the war, so painful to even think about; he would bury his face against Nina's shoulder and breathe in her smell, so distant and so ardently desired. . . . And there would be no war, no sorrowful, aged eyes, no black string of people straggling across the steppe to freight cars, and there would be no dogs barking. There would be nothing. . . .

"That's Vasilisa's hut over there," said the woman. "Thanks for the soap, soldier. I'm going over to the office to deliver the mail."

Vladimir Nikolaevich went up to the porch. His heart

Comrade Shifrin!

was pounding so hard that he pressed his little suitcase to his chest and stood there panting, as if at the end of a long and arduous ascent. Tap-tap. . .

"Who's there?" came a frightened voice from behind the door.

"Do Nina and Natasha Polyakov live here?" he asked with dead white lips.

There was a gasp from behind the door, the latch opened with a click, and all at once Nina clung silently to his wet overcoat, with its smell of tobacco and railroad station. . . .

"Where do you think you're going?" grumbled old Vasilisa. "It's snowing out there, there's a frost. He could make it without you, you know. She's just like a helpless child. Natasha here is smarter. . . . What, don't you think he can get there by himself?"

Nina was putting Vladimir Nikolaevich's things into his little suitcase. He sat on a bench in his white government-issue undershirt, smoking and watching Natashka. She sat on the floor playing with his canteen, his rifle belt, and his medal "For Combat Services." She was such a quiet, serious child, and this frightened Vladimir Nikolaevich. During those first moments he had hungrily examined the child, with a strange feeling of surprise as he picked out his features in her—the nose, eyes, the way she smiled. Then he had taken the chocolate out of his suitcase and offered it to the little girl. Natasha looked indifferently at the brown bar and put it aside. The medal was much more interesting. Nina glanced apologetically at her husband and said, "Don't be angry, Volodya, she's never seen such a thing before."

They walked to the station. Nina carefully took Vladimir Nikolaevich by the arm and greeted the women who came out of their houses.

Here's to Your Health,

"These are our people, from Moscow," she whispered in Vladimir Nikolaevich's ear. "Marusya's husband was killed."

A young woman in a black shawl caught sight of Vladimir Nikolaevich and turned away. He felt terribly guilty. Here he was, alive and not once wounded, walking with his wife, while Marusya's husband lay somewhere, buried in the earth, never again to see his Marusya.

Nina pressed closer to her husband's shoulder, and they walked along the familiar road to the station.

"Remember when... ? And remember the time... ?" they interrupted each other. They wanted to tell each other everything that had happened, that had remained unsaid, or had already been told to everyone else. In effect, they really didn't know one another, they had invented one another during this difficult wartime separation. Nina hurried on, unable to shake the feeling that this was their last meeting, that she would never again walk side by side with this man in the gray, crumpled overcoat. And then they were silent, each thinking his own thoughts. Vladimir Nikolaevich imagined how he would arrive at his unit and tell the boys —exhausted from their journeys and from longing for women—about his wife, about his daughter, so serious and strange. Nina thought about how she would have to put some potatoes in the oven, or else Natashka would go hungry, and old Vasilisa....

They still had a long way to walk to the station.

... And when Nina would get tired and could go no further, they would find an old haystack, miraculously intact, in a field and crawl up on it. And Nina would fall asleep with her head in his lap, and he would stroke her hair and think, think, recall the past and try to guess the future.

He'd come home from the war, and Nina would meet him at the Belorussian Station. Bands would be playing

Comrade Shifrin!

marches, and the platform would be strewn with flowers. Stalin would be standing at a rostrum, waving a greeting. They would march in formation past a crowd of Muscovites, and Volodka Lebeshev would sing at the top of his voice some unimaginably joyous song for all of Gorky Street to hear, and Natasha would sit on his shoulder and wave a little red flag. . . . If only he managed to stay alive, if only there were no sorrowful eyes and no strings of people straggling towards the freight trains parked on the steppe. If only there were no hungry, doleful dogs howling along the sides of the road; if only there had been no old man with his clinging children, if only there were no Marusya in her black shawl, looking with hatred at soldiers left in one piece by the war. . . .

They still had a long way to walk to the station. . . .

18

To: The Editor-in-Chief
From: Contributor A. Shifrin
Re: Letter received from Cheremushki Civil Registry Office

In answer to your request for an explanation regarding the letter received at the editorial office from the Cheremushki Civil Registry Office of the city of Moscow, I must report the following.

On November 11 of this year, I appeared at the Cheremushki Civil Registry Office as a witness to the formal registration of marriage between my old friend Yuri Abramovich Kadashevich and Elena Isaakovna Shchors. Yuri Abramovich, a Jew according to his passport, could have registered as a Russian at one time—as did everyone who was entitled to. He had that right as the son of a Russian mother. On the other hand, Elena Isaakovna Shchors, a Russian according to her passport, was in fact the granddaughter of Civil War hero Nikolai Shchors, legendary commander, famous also from the song "Bloody tracks cover the thick grass." Shchors's wife in those unforgettable days was Fruma Rostova, whose real surname I do not know.

Comrade Shifrin!

Fruma, a secret policewoman hard as a rock, who smashed counterrevolution like a bedbug in the city of Rostov, which had been entrusted to her for that purpose, nevertheless also managed to give birth to a daughter by N. Shchors. This daughter, Valentina, in turn, grew up and married the physicist Isaak Khalatnikov, at present a corresponding member of the USSR Academy of Sciences. The history of his career is even more instructive, since, living in the city of Kharkov, he was chosen by Academician Landau to study in his seminar. At that time, Landau was troubled by the long list of Jewish surnames which graced the rosters of his classes. When he came across the name Khalatnikov, it caused him to think, erroneously, that he would be able to dilute the ranks of theoretical physics with at least one Russian, something the Party and the government had more than once requested. You can imagine how Landau took his mother's name in vain when he found out that this Kharkov Khalatnikov was no straightforward Khalatnikov at all, but an Isaak Markovich Khalatnikov. But it was too late. From the union of Khalatnikov and Valya Shchors there issued a daughter, Lena, who is registered as a Russian in honor of Civil War hero Nikolai Shchors.

Before directly describing all that went on in the Cheremushki Civil Registry Office, I must return for a moment to Grandma Fruma Shchors. When she met me two years ago—I had gone to her "government house" at Number Three Serafimovich Street—she made a remark which has dogged me ever since. This remark sounds somewhat menacing, but considering that these are different times, I can relate it to you. She said to me at that time and repeated each time thereafter we met, including at the wedding of Yuri Abramovich Kadashevich and Elena Isaakovna Shchors: "If you had crossed my path in 1918, I would have bumped you off." I think there is no need to ex-

147

Here's to Your Health,

plain that the expression "bump off" was taken by Grandma Shchors from secret police slang of the Civil War period and meant the same thing as what we now understand by the terms "kill," "annihilate," "execute by firing squad." In a word, "bump off." This was said at the dinner table in response to a polemical remark made during my analysis of the current international situation, viz., "Mama, Kolya was wrong."

"What Kolya?" Fruma Shchors asked suspiciously.

"Kolya Shchors," I said, pointing to the portrait of the Civil War hero, an oil painting six feet high and four feet wide, hanging on the wall.

"What do you mean, he was wrong?" Fruma asked, with the above-mentioned remark already forming in her mind.

"Because Kolya," I said, "would simply have taken up a sharp sword and hacked away at all his kin whose ears were adorned with sparkling diamonds, so long as the workers and peasants did not have diamonds to stick in their ears. Instead, these same workers and peasants, for whom Kolya gave his young life, come into Moscow's railroad stations at the rate of a million a day and flow out along the broad avenues of the capital of our homeland in the hopes of buying food and consumer goods to take back to their towns and villages—where it is impossible to get all these things."

Of course, I could have taken back these words and not gotten under Fruma Shchors's skin—Fruma Shchors, who, receiving a special government pension due old Bolsheviks, might not have been aware of these petty, post-Revolutionary details of which I informed her. Maybe that is why Fruma told me, "If you had crossed my path in 1918, I would have bumped you off."

Nevertheless, I did not get the least bit angry with her. Last summer, while spending my vacation in Koktebel—that bit of paradise in the Crimea—I introduced Lena Shchors, the granddaughter of Fruma and

Comrade Shifrin!
Nikolai Shchors, to my old friend Yuri Kadashevich. Yuri had arrived in Koktebel announcing that he was too simple and unpretentious and that no pleasures, including sexual ones, interested him, and that at present his happiness was enhanced only by vacuous high society chatter and casual encounters.

Then I brought him Lena Shchors in her elegant white tennis outfit, and I said to Kadashevich that precisely this girl would fit in with his second objective. She stood there, slim, suntanned, holding a foreign Dunhill racket. This tennis racket had been bought with certificates in a Beryozka store.

Here I must explain. "Certificates" are special money given to certain higher-ranking comrades who have received the right to travel abroad and who bring back foreign currency. This currency must be turned in to a special bank in exchange for "certificates." With these, one can go into special stores with the pretty Russian name "Beryozka" and buy elegant foreign blouses, umbrellas, tasty sweets, caviar produced especially for foreigners, and choice sausage made in a special section of the A. I. Mikoyan Meat-Packing Plant. I have an idea that this sausage must be different from the sausage that one buys in ordinary delicatessens. Once I heard the wife of a Party worker say to the wife of another Party worker, "Yesterday my Vanya ate some kind of local sausage and got sick." This meant that Vanya's wife had accidentally bought some ordinary delicatessen sausage. Vanya's stomach, which was used to Beryozka sausage, took note of the difference. I cannot describe how these wonder-working certificates look because I have never seen one. Unfortunately, they have also never been seen by the millions of passengers who arrive daily at the Square of the Three Railroad Stations in Moscow. On the other hand, had they been seen by these millions, the railroads would not have met their passenger-haulage norms.

Here's to Your Health,

Looking at the life companion I had selected for him, Yuri Abramovich said that he was sufficiently simple and unpretentious to marry the granddaughter of Shchors and the daughter of a member of the Academy of Sciences. After which, Lena said several words that would be inappropriate on this page and about which Yuri said he had never heard a more intriguing and yet natural obscenity, and that this only strengthened the decision he had just made.

Thereupon, Yuri rented a miserable three-ruble-a-day storeroom, which he affectionately referred to by the French term "châlet," and carried off Lena Shchors to the wide bed which occupied seven-eighths of the place.

Later, back in Moscow, the young people I had introduced to one another filed an application in the Cheremushki Civil Registry Office, in order to create a strong communist family, the nucleus of our society. Otherwise, the relations between the above-mentioned young people would have had a spontaneous, unregulated character, which would have elicited the censure of the neighbors, of hero's widow Fruma Shchors, and of Corresponding Member of the USSR Academy of Sciences I. M. Khalatnikov.

On these grounds, on November 11 of this year I appeared in the Cheremushki Civil Registry Office as a witness, accompanying the bride and groom, and carrying a bottle of Soviet champagne procured earlier in Koktebel for the purpose of drinking said champagne subsequent to the marriage ceremony. Approaching the buffet set up on the Civil Registry Office premises, I politely and in a civilized manner asked the waitress to give me four glasses, in order to propose a toast to the health of the young couple. But I was informed that it was forbidden to bring alcoholic beverages into the Civil Registry Office as these were sold in the office itself, and so could be bought there. Then, promising to

Comrade Shifrin!

buy something on the premises, too, I took a false step, announcing that the champagne I had brought was French. Unfortunately, I added, it was not available in an ordinary store and had been brought from Paris especially for my friends' wedding. I understand that here I went too far. I never have been and never will be in Paris—for the reason that this is impossible. But, well acquainted with France from my reading, I nonetheless vividly imagined that I *had* been in Paris and *had* brought back this bottle.

This is explained further by the fact that when we arrived at the Civil Registry Office from the newlyweds' apartment, we had already drunk a few to the health of this strong young family. Perhaps that is why I said my bottle of champagne was French. As Comrade Zotova, manager of the Cheremushki Civil Registry Office, wrote in her complaint, "The French champagne he brought with him later turned out to be Soviet." Although, if one were to yield to the truth of life instead of the truth of fact, this Soviet champagne could easily have been acquired by me in Paris and have been brought back from there for my friends' wedding. Especially as we are establishing excellent economic relations with France, our good friend to the west, and we might well export Soviet champagne to them in return for ore, natural gas, and silicate fertilizers necessary to our agriculture. Of course I could have brought this bottle from France if I had been there; but I had not been there.

Having been refused by the waitress, I looked irritatedly for the Civil Registry Office manager, Comrade Zotova, and asked her help in procuring said glasses. Comrade Zotova explained to me that, according to Moscow City Ordinance Number 576, the carrying in and drinking of said alcoholic beverages in the Civil Registry Office are categorically prohibited. After a marriage ceremony, she said, you may buy wine here and drink to the health of the young couple. And take photographs. Then, I can't deny it, I did the thing that she described in her letter to the editorial office. I took out my work identification card with the gold letters "P-R-E-S-S" and began to wave it slowly in front of her face, saying, "Well, okay, well . . . as an exception, uh, in general, what's the use, it's all in the family. . . ." And I emphasized that in the person of the bride she had the granddaughter of the legendary Shchors. In answer to this, Comrade Zotova, reading in the application that the granddaughter of the legendary Shchors was Isaakovna, did not believe my words and refused to give the glasses. In answer to my witty question—"I wonder whether you exist for the benefit of the newlyweds or the newlyweds for you?"—she said, not catching the sarcasm hidden in my words, that I would have to address that question to a higher authority.

Then I fell back on another maneuver, ignoring the advice of bridegroom Yuri Abramovich Kadashevich, who begged me to be simpler and less pretentious. When they had summoned us all into the hall, and a deputy from the District Soviet, fulfilling the function of the pre-Revolutionary priest, had congratulated Yuri Abramovich and Elena Isaakovna in a warm voice, in the name of the Russian Soviet Federated Socialist Republic, on the formation of a new Soviet family, I butted in and asked the deputy to drink our bottle of French champagne with us in honor of those excellent words which she had just pronounced. The embarrassed deputy went over to the waitress, whose refusal makes me indignant even now, and returned a few minutes later, explaining apologetically that they would not give her any glasses. But, they said, the young people, after registering, could go into the buffet and buy wine there. And take photographs.

Then, unable to restrain myself any longer, I opened the bottle of champagne and all of us—including the

Comrade Shifrin!

deputy, whose ample body was encircled by a scarlet ribbon of watered silk like those worn by American beauty-queens—we all drank the champagne from the bottle, with the bride, now wife Elena Isaakovna Shchors, granddaughter of the Civil War hero, drinking the most, making her husband Yuri Abramovich Kadashevich ecstatic. He shouted, "Just look how simple and unpretentious my Lyonok is!"

We left the Cheremushki Civil Registry Office, and at the exit I promised Comrade Manager Zotova that I would long, long remember her simple sweet face.

In connection with the foregoing, I request that I be forgiven, and that my case not be transmitted to the higher authorities.

Signed,
A. Shifrin
Marriage Witness

19

A WAVE OF "press conferences" swept the country. This is how they worked: at some Party district committee headquarters they would gather together from a previously compiled list some of the best-known Jews, "acknowledged by the Party and the people." These Jews would passionately denounce "the criminal Zionist gang of mercenaries of American imperialism" and explain that neither they—these handpicked Jews—nor their relatives and friends, nor, for that matter, all the other "Soviet people of Jewish nationality," ever dreamed, nor *would* they ever dream, of emigrating to "a fascist-type state"; that is, in plain language, to Israel.

They showed the most interesting snatches of such "press conferences" on television, and everyone could see the pious faces of the orators who, gesticulating and speaking with Jewish accents, assured the Soviet television audiences of their loyalty "to the Communist Party and our own beloved Soviet government." These people were basically always the same: Deputy Chairman of the Council of Ministers Dymshits, Academician Mitin, author Chakovsky, former pilot Gofman, General Dragunsky. Sometimes the cast was diluted by a famous actor or a collective farm chairman. The secret police

Comrade Shifrin!

who attended these "press conferences" looked with revulsion at the flushed faces of the participants, who swore them eternal love and gratitude.

Here's Genrikh Gofman. Pilot. Lieutenant. Hero of the Soviet Union. Bombed Berlin. Later began to write books on military subjects. A good fellow. Most likely a daredevil. I imagined him directing his bomber towards smoldering Berlin and muttering hoarsely, through clenched teeth, "Take that, you fascist bastards, from a Jew. From all Jews. For all the Jews." What on earth had happened to him? Why was he babbling something "in the name of all Soviet people of Jewish nationality?"

Here's the actress Bystritskaya. A beautiful woman. She played Aksinia in the film *Quiet Flows the Don*. My God, she's also Jewish! Who would have suspected it! Yes, she, too, wouldn't go to Israel for anything. And the other Soviet actors of Jewish nationality, they wouldn't go to Israel for anything either. They'd all be delighted to play the role of Aksinia. And other roles, too. That is, if they were to be entrusted with them. Her, they trusted. And she's Jewish. I imagined that this speech was now being heard in Rostov-on-Don by the descendants of the Don Cossacks. They would tear this Bystritskaya beauty to pieces! Just think, their Aksinia, their national heroine, was played by some Yid! So, this is what goes on in the world! Everything is upside-down! Couldn't they find a Russian actress for such an important role? It's beyond human understanding!

And here's the collective farm chairman. He says, "Where, when, in what country could I imagine that I, a simple Jew, could host the General Secretary of the Communist Party of the Soviet Union? Or that he would sit at the same table with me? There is no such country." All in all, he's right. Really. There *is* no such country!

I was casually acquainted with pilot Gofman. We

sometimes drank cognac and beer together in one or another of those "clubs for the creative intelligentsia." One day I was sitting in such a club with some friends. A day or two earlier there had been a "Zionist witches' sabbath" somewhere in Brussels at which our representative, Hero of the Soviet Union Gofman, exposed the cunning plans of the Pentagon, which was trying to sow discord among the peoples of the Soviet Union. He said that, as the song goes, no one is unwelcome at our Soviet table. He said that we live more joyfully each day. He said that people in our country stride like lords across our immense homeland. And in conclusion, he observed that no other country did he know, where men could breathe so deep and free. And Jews, too.

We were drinking cognac as Lieutenant Gofman walked by. He said hello and came over to us.

"So, what's new?" he asked and sat down.

"You know, Gena," I said to him, "when we have our Auschwitz, you'll be a kapo there."

I really didn't mean to offend him. It's not his fault. He's simply no hero. Oh, yes, of course he's a Hero—but of the Soviet Union! A war hero. But in peacetime, it's hard to say who's an enemy and who isn't. Everyone is the enemy. Or everyone is a friend. It depends on which side of the barricade you're on. He looked at me with such pain! He was pale and couldn't say a word.

Neither could I. He suddenly jumped up and ran out.

... Five days later I was summoned by the editor-in-chief.

He called me in to meet with the Party organizer. We were silent until he arrived; the editor clenched and unclenched his jaw and looked down at the table. I was hateful in his eyes.

The Party organizer came in.

"Well, what happened?" I asked as casually as possi-

Comrade Shifrin!

ble. I more or less sensed what had happened. I couldn't help sensing it.

The director began with self-control. "I have just received a call from the Party organizer of the Writers' Union. Comrade Secretary Vasiliev asked us to look into the case of Comrade Shifrin. Several days ago Shifrin informed Hero of the Soviet Union Gofman that in our country we will soon have an Auschwitz and Gofman will be a kapo there. You've done it at last, you phony, you damned grumbler," he began to yell suddenly. "Who's pulling you by the tongue? Are you playing the liberal? I'll throw you off this newspaper in five minutes, and you won't get another job in five years! What do you think you can get away with?"

"Hmm, yes, a serious case," said the Party organizer. "I think we must call a Party meeting. This is very unhealthy talk...."

"Unhealthy? The devil only knows what kind of talk this is!" shouted the director.

"So, he betrayed me after all," I said.

"How dare you use such a word about a Communist!" the director was outraged. "Betrayed! What a word! He didn't *betray* you, he did his duty and told the Party the truth. Or is that beyond your comprehension?"

The wheels started turning. I was finished—*that* I understood—but how could I get out of this with minimal losses?

"Listen," I said, "I was drunk . . ."

"So?"

"And he was also drunk . . ."

"So?"

"We both were drunk . . ."

"So what, God damn it?!"

"In my drunkenness, I said something entirely different to him."

"What did you say to him?"

"I said to him, 'Gena, let's drink a toast that we never have an Auschwitz in our country!'"

"Who told you that we could have an Auschwitz?" roared the editor-in-chief. "Where did you read that we could have such a thing? In what sick dream did you dream this?"

"That is, I didn't say to him that we would have an Auschwitz for sure. I said, approximately, 'Gena, let's drink a toast that there will never be any Auschwitzes —in the whole world!'"

"Uh-huh. And what did you blabber about the kapo?"

"What kapo?"

"About the kapo! About the kapo! You know what kapo!"

"I don't know any such word. . . ."

"Listen, Shifrin, you go pester someone else who knows you less well than I do. You will write me immediately a note explaining your outrageous behavior!"

I started to understand that for some reason they weren't going to throw me out. For that, they didn't need any explanations.

"Yes, this is a serious matter," said the Party organizer, looking intently at the editor-in-chief, trying to figure out what he was driving at. "I think we must have a meeting of the Party bureau. Shifrin has said some unhealthy things. . . ."

"Do it this way," the editor-in-chief said to me. "While we decide what to do with you, you go back to work. And write your explanation."

I went to my office. No, they weren't going to fire me. Something was preventing them—but what? Were they afraid of the publicity? Were they afraid that I would make a scene? That someone would sympathize with me? Incomprehensible. . . .

Five hours later they summoned me again.

Comrade Shifrin!

"So," said the editor-in-chief, "we decided together with the Party bureau, that, first of all, you will apologize to Comrade Gofman for the insult, and, secondly, we are going to lower your position and give you a salary cut for your drunken hooliganism."

"How much?"

"What do you mean, how much?"

"Will you take away . . ."

"Twenty-five rubles a month."

"Well, then tell me," I whispered, "for twenty-five rubles a month, can I tell a son-of-a-bitch that he's a son-of-a-bitch?"

"No!" shouted the editor-in-chief, "not for twenty-five rubles, not for thirty rubles, not for a thousand, do you have the right to do that! You are an employee! What right do you have to your own opinion? Why do you think only of yourself? Why don't you think about your comrades! You could get them into a lot of trouble with your foolish talk!"

"What do my comrades have to do with this?" I asked, surprised.

"Because they are also Jews. JEWS! Do you mean that such a simple thought didn't occur to your feeble brain —which has one convolution, tops!"

"Yes, he's probably right," I thought. "Of course, he's right. I'm a pig. An idiotic, frivolous pig."

And I called Gofman and apologized. "I didn't mean to offend you," I said.

"I waited five days for your apology," he said furiously.

"And on the fifth day . . ."

"And on the fifth day I did my duty! I'm tired of having people spit in my face! If you were in my place . . ."

"Good-bye," I said.

Several months later I went to see the editor-in-chief.
"Well, what is it?"
"I would like to ask you to give me back those twenty-five rubles."
"Why is that, may I ask?"
"I can't make ends meet," I said, handing him a piece of paper with a column of figures on it. "Look. You used to pay me two hundred rubles a month. Now I get one hundred seventy-five. Of that, twenty-five rubles go for income tax. That leaves one hundred fifty. Transportation to and from work? Minus six rubles a month for a commuter ticket. One forty-four. Do I have to eat breakfast every day? Let's say one ruble a day. Minus thirty. That leaves one fourteen. Do I have to eat lunch? Yes. A worker without lunch is not a worker. Let's say one ruble a day. Minus thirty. That leaves eighty-four. Do you eat supper? So do I. Let's say another ruble a day. Minus thirty. That leaves fifty-four. I'm a smoker. Do I have a right to that vice, as a high-paid newspaperman? One pack a day. Forty kopecks a pack. Twelve rubles. That leaves forty-two. Once a week to the laundry, six rubles. That leaves thirty-six. Do I have to pay rent for my apartment? You will agree that under the circumstances it's a good thing that I have a tiny one-room government apartment, and not a two-room co-operative. Because of that, only fourteen rubles. That leaves twenty-two. And gas, electricity, telephone? Minus eight. That leaves fourteen. Do I have to clean my clothes and shoes? I don't work in a boiler room, you know. Minus seven. That leaves seven. And union membership fees? And dues for other social organizations? Minus five. Leaving two. We are both intelligent people. Do we have to go to the movies once a month? Minus one. One ruble left! Am I a Soviet man or not? Do I not have the right to drink a bottle of vodka with my friends at least once a month? Especially since I

Comrade Shifrin!

have all this unpleasantness! I do have the right! And if you add to that one remaining ruble three rubles and twelve kopecks from my personal savings, I can allow myself this luxury. Don't you agree? "And now let's not forget that I have a family. What can I bring home as a husband and father? You see, to put it crudely, I am the breadwinner."

The editor-in-chief looked at me, spellbound, cracking his knuckles.

"So what do you live on?" he asked with obvious interest.

"I don't know," I confessed honestly. "And don't forget that I'm a highly-paid specialist."

The editor-in-chief called in the bookkeeper and said to him, "Give Shifrin back his twenty-five rubles. He has upset me very much." And to me, "But let's have no more Auschwitzes. Is that clear?"

20

"MY YOUNG FRIEND," the editor said to me, "why are you sticking this anti-Soviet stuff under my nose? Do you seriously believe that I would put this little story out on the pages of our newspaper?"

"Of course I do," I said. "Our readers would be very glad to read this witty and truthful story."

"What readers?" the editor asked wearily. "Do you still maintain the illusion that someone reads our newspaper, that we have readers?"

"Yes, of course. Our readers are those who read us."

"Darling," said the editor, "the readers are divided into two unequal parts: those who read us from below—they are the subscribers—and those who read us from above. Those who read us from below, we'll leave them out of this, they should read in peace. That's what we're working for. Let's think about the ones who read us from above. There are six of them all together. Six readers. Imagine that one of them doesn't like this little story here. We'd have to wipe you up with a sponge, my friend. You'd turn into dust. Do you understand? You see, I wouldn't protect you. I'd say that I didn't read this little story. You just sneaked it in! And where would you be then? Besides, I really don't understand why this is

Comrade Shifrin!
so important to you. Why are you asking for trouble?"
"Listen, don't you understand that a person wants to speak the truth?" I said. "That's why we were born."
"So, what will your truth bring you? Are you so sure that people want to read the truth? I'm not. The truth is very inconvenient. Imagine a man has cancer. Are you saying that the doctor should tell him the truth?"
"The doctor should cure him!"
"Alas, my dear, it's not so simple. The doctor should prescribe tasty pills for the patient in order not to scare him or those close to him. And you call for revelation! It's not humane."
"But the patient will die!"
"What can you do? We're not yet immortal. Listen, ideas are immortal, but man, unfortunately, is not. So you don't have to come sneaking up to me with your clever but anti-Soviet little stories."
"But a man can't lie all the time. Your patient is all wrapped in fragrant, pink bandages, but he's rotting. Don't you think it's time to start curing him?"
The editor was playing gloomily with his ball-point pen.
"Some aging young people," he said, "still live with antiquated ideas. With the ideas, say, of the Twentieth Party Congress. God help me, don't think that I'm against them! How could anyone be against them? The cult of personality and all that. . . . But you must have a dialectical approach to life: today we have before us the decisions of the Twenty-fourth Congress! That's what the up-to-date Soviet man must live by. That is, of course, if he doesn't want to have his head handed to him. So take back your little story and don't bother me with it any more."
"Well, that I can't promise you!" I said angrily.
"Why not?"
"Because they haven't bought me yet. I still have the right to my own point of view."

Here's to Your Health,

The editor looked at me ironically and said, "Well, that's very interesting. Let's look at it more closely. So, how much is your point of view worth?"

"As much as yours is worth to you."

"Well, how much is that?"

"If you please," I said. "A personal expense allowance—one! Special canteen privileges—two! Government apartment—three! A special bonus—four! Free holidays at health resorts—five! A special medical clinic—six! Special hospital care—seven! Personal summer dacha—eight! Personal car—nine! Three-month paid vacation—ten! The green light for my stories in a literary journal—eleven! Yearly trips to capitalist countries—twelve! And a few incentives in sealed envelopes—thirteen! What else?"

"That's enough," the editor said softly. "That's too expensive, my dear. You have to earn all that. So, for the time being, stay where you are with your wonderful truth, and I'll stay where I am with my falsehood. Okay? But all the same, you're still working for me. So now I'll teach you our basic requirements for literary works, and you will observe them. Otherwise, no matter how much I might regret it, we'll have to part company. I like you, you have the youthful enthusiasm of a Komsomol member. You have a lot of spunk. Ah, youth, youth . . ."

The editor was lost in thought for a long time.

"So," he began again. "All members of the press are divided into two groups of unequal size. The first group is composed of people who are sympathetic to the social ideas which arose in the country as a result of the Twentieth Congress of the Communist Party. People like you, my young friend. They want to use our pages to publish and push through the works of so-called 'honest' (you see, I'm not afraid of such a word) writers and journalists who point out the faults of our system or who

Comrade Shifrin!

try to reform our governmental and economic institutions.

"These are to be contrasted with the second, much more numerous, group of people, whose task it is to keep such materials from being published. Naturally, I belong to the second group.

"So. I have special obligations, and I am responsible to the Central Committee of the Communist Party for the ideas issuing from my editorial office. In turn, I lay such obligations on everyone who works under me. Of course, different people have different degrees of political maturity. Here you, friend, can't stand a simple test of political maturity, and I, with all my personal sympathy for you, should have shown you the door long ago. But I want to change your views. It still seems to me that you'll come around, that you're not yet beyond hope.

"To continue. Each member of the press must also function as a censor. What does this mean?

"Isn't there something in the author's material that could be taken two ways? For instance, in your story, one finds the aphorism 'the line gets shorter if you close ranks.' This is a hint at the long waiting-lines in our stores. And a parody of the Party slogan 'if you close ranks!' Of course, this little sentence has no place in our —yours and mine—newspaper.

"Isn't there some hint about the existence of a generation gap?

"Isn't there some hint about unresolved international problems?

"Isn't there some hint about serious economic difficulties?

"Aren't there unnecessary generalizations?

"Isn't there a predominantly negative attitude towards life?

"Where is the life-affirming humor? Note, I said life-affirming—that is, affirming *our* life!

"Aren't there hints that the Party's general policy is wrong?

"Don't the parodies and satirical articles insult, God forbid, government or Party leaders, recognized authors, heads of central public and other organizations, et cetera?

"Isn't there some criticism of the working class and the collective farm peasantry?

"Isn't there criticism of the government apparatus?

"Isn't there hidden support for dissidents?

"Doesn't the discussion of certain problems echo certain claims made by Western radio stations broadcasting to the Soviet Union?

"Isn't there a preponderance of Jewish names on the pages?"

"And why is that a problem?" I asked.

"I hope you don't think I'm an anti-Semite?"

"Hmmm . . ."

"You're mooing in vain; you know very well that I'm not. But consider for yourself—if in a Moscow newspaper you read only, let's say, Uzbek names, wouldn't you think it was strange?"

"If these were talented writers . . ."

"Don't fool yourself, my dear, it *would* seem strange. And if all you see is Bermans, Ofshteins, Shteinboks, Livshitses, and Levenbukhs, isn't that strange? . . . You're not getting bored, are you?"

"No, go ahead . . ."

"To resume. Isn't there a hint of discord between the Party and the people?

"Isn't there a hint about the lack of correspondence between Party slogans and their execution?

"Isn't there a suggestion that the Central Committee is returning to Stalinism?

"Is the status quo observed?"

"What's that?"

Comrade Shifrin!

"See how inexperienced you are. As is well known, the Party, actively trying to influence life, turned its actions some time ago against so-called 'left' groups. 'Right-wingers' were more or less forgotten. For instance, you might very well see criticism of 'cosmopolitans' or 'young prose,' but no mention at all of such writers as Kochetov or Shevtsov. Misled, maybe, but our own. Today, alongside criticism of 'leftists' it's not a bad idea to draw some blood (figuratively speaking, of course) from assorted 'patriots' of old peasant Russia, as well as from anti-intellectuals and other enemies of technological progress. Do you understand me? This is what I call observance of the status quo.

"So, when any member of the press, including myself, of course, can answer all these questions in the sense required of us, then the newspaper comes out, to the delight of its readers and admirers."

We were silent. The editor smiled and looked me in the eye.

"You know, chief," I said. "You're a wise and intelligent man. Why do you find it more interesting to live like this, and not in some other way? I can well imagine that you go home after work, close the shutters, lie down in bed, cover your head with a blanket, and read Gumilyov's poetry by flashlight, so nobody can see you."

"Very imaginative, my dear boy," said the editor. "That's exactly what I do. And I advise you to do the same."

I wanted to be able to picture how this man became who he was. How they all became like that. I said to him, "I have this picture in front of me, chief. They call you before Comrade X in a big building on an old Moscow square. You don't know why they've called you. You're worried. You're nervous. They don't just summon people like that. Something's probably happened. You try to remember all your mistakes of the last month. The last year. Five years. Your whole life. You must have done something sometime. Or wanted to do something. Or someone thought that you wanted to do something. Or someone thought that you were capable of doing something.

"You arrive at the reception room at precisely the appointed time. The military man at the entrance is somehow particularly careful in checking over your documents. Several times he looks tentatively from the photograph on your papers to your face and back. His eyes are calm and merciless. At last he says, 'Please!' And you pass into the reception room. There are no visitors there. You are alone. You sit down carefully on the edge of a leather sofa, and you wait. You wait an hour. Two hours. Three. No one. The door through which you entered automatically slammed shut behind you. A thousand thoughts split your head. And all of a sudden a young, disciplined military man appears as if from out of the ground and says politely (too politely, it seems to you), 'Please follow me.'

"You walk down a long, clean corridor towards an enormous unmarked double door.

"The young man opens the door and, with a nod, invites you to enter.

"You pass through the doors, which close silently behind you, and you find yourself in a huge room. A white room. And the ceiling and floor are also white. The windows are hung with white curtains. At first it seems as if the room is completely empty, but then in the distance you notice a desk with a man bent over it. He's writing something. He doesn't notice you. You walk slowly towards the desk as if you were crossing a field. You feel empty and alone. The man lifts his head, smiles, and adjusts his gold-rimmed glasses. He stands up, walks around his enormous desk (only after crossing the room did you see that the desk was enormous), and walks towards you. He firmly grasps your hand. You

Comrade Shifrin!

sigh, relieved, and the weight you were carrying in your heart for all those days before this meeting begins to lift. The man takes you by the arm and you stroll around this white room, and he says to you, quietly and sincerely, 'How good that you came, my friend! If you only knew how we need your help. Look what's going on in the world! We're surrounded by enemies. It is difficult for us to work. Our youth are poisoned by foreign influences. The peasants don't work. The workers don't want to increase their productivity. And our intelligentsia is responsible for all of this. You'd think they were lacking something. We've created the best conditions in the world for them, and all the same they're not with us. . . . You must help us. . . .'

"You walk with him along the white walls, and the man talks and talks, quietly and confidently. Then he presses a tiny white button and a small, iron door in the wall opens silently. And you see everything that's happening beyond that door. And the man keeps on talking about faith, about the enemies' intrigues, about the future, about the past, and about your enormous responsibility. And you keep looking there, through the secret door in the white wall. . . . And what you see there will remain in your memory throughout your life! Throughout your whole life!

"Then the door closes slowly and silently, and the man accompanies you to the threshhold, shakes your hand, and says that he's sure of you, one of the best people he's ever had the good fortune to meet.

"What did you see there, chief, beyond the small iron door in the wall? What did you see there?"

The editor, suddenly looking old and tired, murmured, "Go back to your office, my friend. For some reason, I'm not feeling very well today."

21

"Shifrin, how would you like to travel abroad?"
"Excuse me, I didn't hear you right. . . ."
"Don't be cute, I'm serious. There are trips to Bulgaria. Tourist trips. Cheap. For active Komsomol members."
"Oh, what the devil. Why not? Why shouldn't I see the world?"

When I was a child my mother used to read me these verses:

> I'll never see the Amazon,
> So far away from here.

When I grew up, I found out that this was Kipling.
Later I found out about many other poets and writers. I witnessed fierce literary battles. The ungifted always destroyed the gifted. The gifted ones were flabby intellectuals—and the methods of the ungifted were repugnant to them. So they were always defeated. The ungifted were muscular and ignorant. They attacked in closed ranks. They labeled the gifted with "isms" and tormented them. The gifted kept silent. Some of them

Comrade Shifrin!

couldn't stand it and started to write like the ungifted. Then the ungifted would say, "See, he can, but he doesn't want to! See, he can do it, the son-of-a-bitch, when he wants to." I knew many poets and writers. . . . All kinds.

Years later I still remember, with unexplainable longing, the Kipling verses my mother read to me when I was little:

> Will I ever see Brazilia,
> Brazilia, Brazilia,
> Will I ever see Brazilia,
> Just once before I die?

Later, to forestall annoying questions from my acquaintances, I invented a mythical fiancée who was living in Africa.

"Why aren't you married yet, friend?" my acquaintances would ask me every day. "It's not healthy to be alone." And they would make faces as if I were the worst sex maniac in the city. I got sick and tired of this question. I couldn't explain to them that I simply didn't have a girl, that I wasn't in love, and that I couldn't marry just anyone. I would say to them, "Look, this is a very tragic story. My fiancée lives in Africa."

"In Africa?!" my acquaintances would exclaim in surprise.

"Yes, in Africa," I said sadly. "She's sitting in Africa under a palm tree, eating coconuts and pining away for love of me. First chance I get, I'll buy a ticket, fly to Africa, and bring her home. We'll settle down in Zhmerinka."

"Go to hell!" my acquaintances would spit. But those whom I managed to tell about the palm tree didn't pester me any more.

At last, it really did begin to seem to me that my

intended lived somewhere far, far away, and that she, lonely and sad, was telling her friends across the sea about her fiancé, who was sitting under a branching cranberry tree in far-off, cold Russia.

"Well, so what, Bulgaria isn't Africa, but it's also the world," I thought. "I'll go to Bulgaria." The only thing I knew about Bulgaria was what every Soviet citizen knows, namely—"Bulgaria is a good country, but Russia is the best."

"We'll see," I decided. I handed in all my papers, went through all the clearance procedures, collected all my character references and applications, and took off for Europe with a group of Komsomol activists.

We were a large group, about twenty people. Our leader was a Comrade Shishkov, a gloomy and suspicious young man who looked like the actor Fait. His right-hand man was a kid I nicknamed "our trusty helper the Shadow." They were serious and vigilant men.

"The main thing is order," our leader loved to say. "The main thing is not to wander off, but for all to keep together." He counted us like chicks, and the Shadow brought up the rear.

"Everyone's here!" he would shout. "Let's go!"

Bulgaria impressed me. It was a beautiful and hospitable country. They loved Russia in Bulgaria, loved Russia because of the liberation from the Turks, because we were neighbors, because we were Slavs. The sidewalks of Sofia were paved with yellow stone. In the evening the citizens filled the restaurants and cafés. They came with their families, drank beer, ate chops big as round loaves of bread, and sang along with the orchestra playing quietly in the corner. Children came, too. They sat sedately at the table and drank lemonade through a straw.

I had my first run-in with Comrade Shishkov over an incident in the picture gallery.

Comrade Shifrin!

"Just look at this scribble," said the Shadow. "They call this art? My little brother Kolka, he's five years old, he could draw better than that."

"No, my friend," I said, "your Kolka can't draw like that."

"What, this smear?" the Shadow countered with surprise.

And then I put my foot in it. Like a fool, I started to explain to the Shadow why his brother Kolka couldn't create anything like that painting. I explained that one had to study, that painting was as difficult to understand as symphonic music, that this wasn't scribbling. . . .

"So," said the Shadow, "I see . . . So, you're defending them?"

"Who?"

"You know who," he uttered menacingly, and went off to whisper with Comrade Shishkov.

"Excuse me," the tour guide said to me, "but I accidentally overheard your interesting discussion." She smiled. "If you have time, I'd like to show you something."

She took me aside to a storeroom and showed me several more pictures. And although they didn't seem entirely original, I nevertheless praised them. She was very pleased; I could see by her face that she didn't often have the opportunity to talk about art, and here was someone who agreed with her—and from Russia, at that.

In the hotel, Comrade Shishkov said, "I don't like these conversations, Shifrin. You want to be smart, eh? 'I understand, but you plebeians don't understand.' Right? You're trying to be unique, right?"

"What are you talking about?" I said. "It's just that the Shadow is insensitive to art. It doesn't threaten him."

"Hmmm," said Comrade Shishkov. "Remember what I told you. . . ."

Our group translator was a Bulgarian girl named Pavlina. She was studying in the Russian department of the university. We were lying side-by-side on the beach, on the Golden Coast near Varna, enjoying a rest. Before this we had taken a trip to a collective farm . . .

. . . After the kolkhoz chairman had told us about their successes and had introduced us to the members of the village soviet, I stood up (Comrade Shishkov had given me this task) and said, "We like it here very much. We like the fact that there are many young people in the fields. We like the fact that you are well-dressed, and that your village has a restaurant and a museum. We like your faith in the future. We are glad that you live well. I propose a mental toast to the friendship of our peoples!"

"Why mental?" exclaimed the chairman. He clapped his hands, the doors opened, and red-cheeked, black-eyed Bulgarian girls dressed in national costume brought in wine and appetizers. Frankly, we were starved. . . .

Bulgarian *slivovitsa* has the properties of napalm: if you exhale, every living thing within a twenty-yard radius goes up in flames.

The collective farmers neatly gathered up our picturesquely sprawling bodies and carried them carefully to the bus.

"Good-bye, good-bye."

One of my eyes was sleeping, while the other watched the peasants crowded in front of the village soviet waving good-bye to us with kerchiefs and hats, until our bus passed out of sight around a dusty bend. . . .

So we were lying on the Golden Coast beach enjoying the quiet.

"Tell me, Tolya," Pavlina was saying to me, "why are

Comrade Shifrin! you Russians so suspicious? Why do you sometimes say one thing and think something entirely different?"

"You're wrong, Pavlinochka," I said, thinking of something else that was on my mind. "We're not like that. We're straightforward fellows, we say what's on our mind!"

"That's not true, Tolya," she said, getting angry. "Take Comrade Shishkov, for example. He looks like a Spartan, but last night he dropped some strange hints to me, and when I told him that he must be joking, he said he'd write a letter about me reporting that I had behaved badly with the delegation."

"He's a scoundrel, Pavlinochka," I said, "a scoundrel and a bastard. . . ."

I heard a rustling noise behind me, and the trusty Shadow popped out of the bushes. "So, you're spreading propaganda, counterrevolutionary! Maligning the Soviet people? All right . . ."

That evening there was a trial.

The "troika" was assembled in a tent. Comrade Shishkov, the Shadow, and my tent-mate Lyoshka Spassky sat behind a table. Comrade Shishkov announced, "We have before us a person who has forgotten that he is a representative of our great country. A few days ago, in the museum, he defended abstract art. Today he has brought shame on his comrades. I propose that he be sent back home at once and that the appropriate organizations be informed of this incident. Shall we vote?"

"Absolutely right," said the Shadow.

"Why are you keeping quiet, Lyoshka?" I asked my tent-mate. "Say something."

Lyoshka looked away. He lowered his eyes and raised his hand.

I was scared. God, how scared I was! I shook with fright. What was going to happen to me? If they kicked me out of the group, there'd be no place for me anywhere! I imagined myself . . . Fear was written all over my face. They glared at me in triumph.

"Forgive me," I whispered. "I acted badly and stupidly. Forgive me . . ."

"No!" thundered Comrade Shishkov. I walked out of the tent and staggered into the woods. Better to hang myself! My tongue should only dry up and drop off. Who asked me to get mixed up in their affairs? Sit down and shut up. Now I've really ruined my life! What am I going to do? Fall at their feet, repent? And where is my self-respect? To hell, to hell with self-respect! I groaned loudly.

The rest of our group came out of their tents. They stood there, following me with their eyes. I was completely alone. I understood how frightening it was to be alone. I understood that I was wrong and Comrade Shishkov was right. And I'll never forget how sickening it was to feel guilty for having done the right thing. And I understood those people who wrote their own fatal confessions in thirty-seven, putting their signatures to falsehoods. They were possessed by fear.

In the morning Comrade Shishkov said, "We discussed your behavior at the group meeting and decided that you will finish out the trip with us, and when we get back to Moscow, we will send an account of your behavior to the proper place."

"Thank you," I whispered, "thank you. . . ."

. . . Our train arrived in Ungeny, a station on the Rumanian-Soviet border. We were home. I felt awful.

"Greetings, Motherland!" shouted Comrade Shishkov. He grabbed the Shadow and they ran into the dining car. Then they disappeared into their compartment, bottles hidden under their jackets. Soon songs, shouts, and laughter were heard from their compartment. Then everything was quiet.

"Greetings, Motherland," I thought sorrowfully. "What do you have in store for me?"

Comrade Shifrin!

At the border they added another car to the train. This was some very important Party official returning from abroad. He rode in a separate, guarded car. The people who were accompanying him made the rounds of the train, and, as ours was the last car, they occupied the end compartment. I looked at them. Suddenly I had a brainstorm. I decided to get my revenge on Comrade Shishkov. I decided to put him in my shoes. I wanted him to understand what fear was.

I let my friend, the cameraman Vadka Kruglov, in on my plan and set to work. I opened the door of their compartment and woke up Comrade Shishkov and the Shadow, both of whom were in a drunken stupor.

"What, what?" they said hoarsely.

"What's the matter with you guys?" I whispered. "Couldn't you wait until we got to Moscow?"

"What's going on?"

"Trouble.... You were drinking in here..."

"So?"

"So.... No good came of it...."

"What happened?"

"Yes... well, you were drinking, you started yelling ... all sorts of slogans ... jokes...."

"Cut it out!"

"What, should I repeat what you said?"

And suddenly Comrade Shishkov gasped, "That won't be necessary."

"And now they've added a car with Comrade N ... Security ... Military ... They heard what you were yelling in here and asked me who those people were. Well, I couldn't refuse to tell them. I gave your names. ... They wrote them down ... that's it."

They turned green as grass. They looked uncomprehendingly at one another and tried to smile.

"An unpleasant business," I said.

Vadka Kruglov came in.

"Yeah, guys, you're in for it," he said seriously. "A

177

terrible story. The colonel is sitting over there madder than the devil. He's going to give it to you! What could Tolka do? He said . . ."

"You're lying!" said Comrade Shishkov in despair. "You're lying! It can't be so. I'm going to find out. . . ."

I was hanging by a thread.

"What's he going to tell you?" I said as casually as I could. "He's on duty. He'll tell you, 'That's okay, that's okay, everything's all right,' but he has your names down on paper."

Comrade Shishkov no longer looked like the actor Fait; he resembled a wet chicken. The Shadow was swaying back and forth. He had completely sobered up and was staring at me and Vadka with eyes popping. He seemed not to understand a word.

Comrade Shishkov took action. He went into the compartment where our "colonels" were sitting and said to one of them, "Excuse me, we were drinking a little bit, we just returned home, and, . . . you see . . ."

"That's okay, that's okay, everything's all right," smiled the "colonel."

I felt a weight lift from me. Comrade Shishkov hadn't expected *that* sentence. He made his way to his compartment like a blind man and locked the door behind him.

Vadka said, "Look how they've gone to pieces."

"Of course."

"What shook them up so much?"

"They're double dealers. They can dish it out, but they can't take it."

A half hour later I looked in on them.

"Look," I said, "I'll try to make excuses to the colonel. I think he'll listen to me."

"Please, Tolya," they whined, "you know what could happen. . . ."

"I certainly do. . . ."

Comrade Shifrin!

I went into the compartment of my fake "colonel" and offered to play a game of chess with him. He checkmated me, I thanked him, wrote the names of Comrade Shishkov and his trusty helper the Shadow on a piece of paper, went into the compartment where our leaders were dying of fright and suspense, and threw the paper on the table.

"Thank you, Motherland!" I looked out the window and smoked a cigarette. Past me floated the white Moscow birches, settlements of summer houses, and little streams. . . .

Will I ever see Brazilia,
Brazilia, Brazilia,
Will I ever see Brazilia,
Just once before I die?

Some Comments from Shifrin's Readers

The First Reader

"WELL, WHAT can I tell you? A clever head was given to a fool, that's what I'll tell you. . . . You sit and sit, write and write, and what's the point? . . . Who'd print that nonsense? You criticize everything. And who needs your criticism? Since when are you a critic? If I had such talent, to scratch on paper, you know what I'd do? Make money! You're still young. What do you know about money? . . . You're being a fool with this mangy little book of yours. Do you think no one will catch on?

"So, we come to your house to visit—I even bankrupt myself and take a taxi on such a special occasion. . . . Keep the change, chief.

"What floor are you on? The third? Not so bad.

"You have to upholster your door with leatherette, otherwise you know how the acoustics will be. You sneeze and your neighbor says 'Gesundheit.' Ha-ha-ha. You have an inside toilet? Hmmm. One room? One . . . So . . . Do you live well? You're lying. You live badly. Listen to me, I'm telling you as a friend, you live poorly. And why, do you know? A clever head was given to a fool. Here you write, you don't like this, you don't like that . . . And what *do* you like? The Soviet government? Of course, I know you like it. So why do you get in our way? You're inviting criticism. You want anarchy? You don't? What are you writing, then? Do you know how you ought to write? Most likely, you're sick at heart, you saw something bad. . . . So, blockhead, sit and write a letter of complaint. Go straight to the top. This happened, tell them, and that. I'm sick at heart, tell them, I propose doing such-and-such. They can figure it out. And they'll thank you, you fool. And if you write an intelligent report, they'll take you on to help them. And they'll say, 'He's got a good head, give him a salary so he won't think about anything else. And give him a car so his precious legs don't get tired out on the trolley. He's a young man, married, children will come along, how can he live with a family in one room? Give him an apartment with a room for a nursemaid. Then you've become a man. And then it would be a pleasure to look at you. You see? You don't have to scribble these little books. Otherwise, who are you? Tfu, a zero. If I had your talent . . .

"Why do you mess around with politics? And such politics! You're always rubbing our nose in the dirt. Who likes that? You should say 'Thank you.' Learn this —say 'Thank you' to everything! You say 'Thank you' to us and we won't forget you. Conscience? What does conscience have to do with it? You're still young. . . . It's hard to talk to you. You don't understand the simplest things. . . .

"So what are you now? A gnat . . . A gnat is not supposed to have a conscience. . . . You don't have the right to a conscience yet. First stand on your own two feet. Earn the respect of the government, the leadership, and then carry on later as much as you like. If you want to play conscience, play; if you don't want to play, forget it. All this is sentimentalism . . . and you can't put sentimentalism in your pocket. You can't make a soup from it. A friend comes to your house, and you don't even have a bottle on the table. Don't worry, I under-

Comrade Shifrin!
stand everything. The end of the month, you can't make ends meet. . . . Right? But life means being able to give your friend a bottle any time and not worry about what's left for tomorrow. That's where your conscience gets you. That's your sentimentalism for you. Well, well, so here's a bottle after all. Good for you! But it's not you—it's your wife who's to thank. Here's to your health!

"You're a grumbler, my friend. Everything's wrong as far as you're concerned. What's good for us isn't good for you. And we don't like that. And you raise questions in your little book that you don't understand. Isn't that so? Because great men must solve such problems, and not you and I, little bugs. Oh, but you're cle-e-e-ver! Not a word about Stalin . . . , but Stalin stands behind every line. You phony! You all jumped on Stalin, and what do you think you'll get out of it? Not a thing. Because Stalin did a lot of good things. Hm, hm, he's starting to smile with his little eyes. . . . Don't smile—listen to more intelligent people. Stalin will still make himself felt. Do you think you can manage without Stalin? Like hell you can. It would be too much for you without Stalin. There'd be no order! Here you are wasting paper—burying Stalin. Watch out—you'll wise up one day, and then you'll shed a few tears. . . .

"Life—it has only one truth. Two truths there can't be. Right? So! Here's to your health! You lousy intellectuals—you invent your own new truth at every opportunity. And where does it get you? You ever been in Siberia? I guarded SS-men there. What a life we had. . . . We lived in harmony with them for two years. They knew what discipline meant. Here's to your health! . . . No, my friend, with your talent—make money. Money gives you independence. But you have to write the truth, the truth! And the truth is whatever the people and the Party respect. You go against the people, the Party, and they'll make flour out of you. You got

Here's to Your Health,

that? Here's to your health! So . . . drop this business. . . . We'll be your . . . After all, you're really not a bad sort! Don't be a coward. . . . We'll . . . Here's to your health!"

The Second Reader

"I HAVE A complex reaction to what I read. From my point of view, you have framed the question from a somewhat unusual perspective. And then such a sharp focus. . . . And why did you have to exaggerate an already complex problem? Well . . . , this question . . . Well, you understand. . . . We finished with this long ago, thank God, isn't that so? Well, not completely finished, perhaps, but now this has become, to some degree, the past, isn't that so? In your place I would have somehow soft-pedaled this subject. Is it really so necessary to stir up people all over again?

"And then—our economic problems. Can it really be like this? I perceived this as something of a caricature. Well, of course, of course, not a mirror, but a magnifying glass, of course! But, do you see, this casts a shadow of doubt on many other things as well. . . . Yes, I do remember very well Marx's dictum, 'Doubt everything,' but, you'll forgive me, not to such a degree. This seems to me highly improbable. And to treat our village life the way you treated it, this is quite intolerable! Yes, of course, mistakes were made. . . . But the essential thing has not been lost, has it?

"And this trip abroad . . . It is very unpleasant that

you've described the comrades accompanying the delegation in such a strange manner. It is quite possible that among them there are a few people who were not, should we say, intellectual, but the majority of them are very, very respected comrades with a great deal of work experience, isn't that so?

"And the main thing—your hero . . . Oh, my dear man, what an unusually unattractive hero you have! Even the word 'hero' doesn't suit him, somehow. Well, and what kind of hero is this? He is most uncharming, passive, a drifter, so to speak, carried by the whim of the waves. . . . Yes, I readily concede that such people do actually exist, but why drag them into literature? Literature, in essence, is an instructive, should we say, probing investigation of the heroic personality. There is no lack of examples. . . . Oh, let's say, Pavka Korchagin, Ostrovsky's hero. An upright Communist. An excellent specimen for emulation, wouldn't you say? And all of Russian classical literature. What? Anna Karenina? In what sense? Oh, for emulation? Well, of course it wouldn't do to emulate her in the direct sense of the term, but her image, so to speak. . . . Who? I myself? Well, of course, to some degree I also try to emulate. . . . Pavka Korchagin? Well . . . , to some degree. . . . Well, not literally, of course. Does it make sense to emulate literary heroes? An interesting question. And who should we emulate? What do you mean, why emulate? I don't understand. . . . The whole history of our literature. . . . Why, of course I understand that it's better to emulate live people than literary characters conjured up by writers. But then, allow me to ask you, what is literature's *raison d'être?* In any case, it should direct me. I come home, take a book in my hands, and . . .

"No, no, you haven't convinced me. Let's return to your hero. Why is he so . . . , how shall I say it, not a fighter? What do you mean, who should he fight with?

Comrade Shifrin!

With evil, of course! I can't imagine myself in your hero's place, his passivity. . . . The cult of personality? Oh, you know, this sort of talk has simply become a fad. Hardly such a big thing, the cult of personality. Strictly *entre nous,* it seems to me that here we have already gone too far. The devil isn't all that frightening. . . . And then, this is wearying—to be constantly reading about the seamy side of life. I decisively favor depicting the bright, positive aspects of life. This imparts cheerfulness, spiritual health; it makes life, should we say, more attractive. And you exaggerate. You exaggerate, my boy, you definitely exaggerate. All in all, there isn't so much darkness in life. Why should we bother ourselves about all this? Literature should comfort. And affirm! After all that we have been through, it's absurd, in my opinion, to return again to these subjects. Let bygones be bygones! He who dredges up the past. . . .

"Come on, write a comedy instead: light, sparkling, full of bright humor, without any of those ideas. Just an entertaining comedy. A comedy, my friend, a comedy! All decent people would be in your debt. And think a little less about all these frightening things. They are not the most important thing! By no means! And let your comedy have a hero—young, muscular, brave, strong, in short—an individual, you understand? And let him have some difficulties to surmount. Any difficulties! That's the kind of hero we need. And for such a work, everyone will thank you."

The Third Reader

"I READ IT, of course I read it. . . . Not very carefully, I have a lot to do—but still I read it. Now excuse me, I have to put this pot on the stove.

"It's a shame you wrote so little about love. That always makes it interesting. . . . When I got to the part where the boy in the trolleybus fell in love with the girl, I recalled my own life. My Lyoshka was like that. He noticed me in the subway. Which station? What are you talking about?! In those days there were no stations. They were digging then. A mine shaft. From Sokolniki to the park. I was driving a cart. Oh, we were all so funny! Komsomol kids! At the service of the Komsomol. I was just a teen-ager then, so mischievous . . . , just terrible! And Lyoshka worked in the Komsomol district committee. He was always making speeches. He made beautiful speeches: 'Give the country of the Soviets,' he says, 'a subway!' We registered to be married, bought a kerosene stove, a cupboard, a folding bed . . . Oh, excuse me, I'll move an armchair over here . . .

"So . . . Lyosha was working a lot then. Then, it wasn't like nowadays, you know, a bell rings, and your work is over. In those days, whatever was needed, we worked as long as it took. Lyosha came home from work just

Comrade Shifrin!

black with anger. 'You know, Katya,' he says, 'it's impossible, there are so many saboteurs around! Like mushrooms they grow. You pick some and others pop up. Some kind of ring. And it's all international capitalism!' Once he came home looking like a thundercloud. 'You know,' he says, 'Kolka Vorobyov also turned out to be a saboteur. An enemy of the people. Today they arrested him. . . .' I say, 'Lyoshenka, this can't be! We know Kolka like the palm of our hand. We saw him grow up from a baby right before our eyes. You spent your life together. Why should he be a saboteur? And what do you really think about it?' Lyoshka says, 'This business isn't for us to figure out. They don't arrest people here for nothing. I overlooked Kolka. And because of him, the scoundrel, they might just take away my Party card. And without the Party, there's no way for me to live in this world.' I say, 'How is Rakhil going to live now, without Kolka? She won't be able to stand this.' And Lyosha says, 'Stop this talk. And don't let Rakhil come over here any more. She doesn't have any business here. She's not a fit friend for you. . . .'

"Then the war started. Lyosha got an exemption, of course. Don't think he was some kind of coward. He has decorations. Why, they covered his whole chest so, he had no more room to hang them. And he's a good worker. Where didn't they send him! He worked everywhere. In grain requisitions, and in personnel, in publishing houses, in science, he even worked in films. In your book you wrote about college. Lyosha also worked in a college; he was head of the personnel office. Oh, how he wore himself out over the students. You yourself know what kind of times those were. You had to check everyone very carefully. After the war—many came back from POW camps. Some had been in Nazi-occupied territory. The children of the enemies of the people had grown up. . . . Like what you wrote about. And Lyosha had to answer for everything. And then

Here's to Your Health,

Rakhil Mikhailovna comes to me—Kolya Vorobyov's wife. 'Katenka,' she says, 'talk with your husband . . . , why didn't they accept my Sashka . . . , he has to study . . . , take pity on the boy. My Kolya,' she says, 'never came back. Sashka is all I have.' I told Lyoshka. He got stern and says, 'Katya,' he says, 'don't meddle in these matters, you don't understand anything. This business isn't for us to figure out. If they didn't accept him, that means that's the way it should be. And don't speak to me about this any more.' Well, all right.

"And then Stalin died. My God, how we mourned him. Lyoshka was grief-stricken, he cried like a baby. 'How are we going to live now?' he says. 'Russia can't live without Stalin. Everything in the world is connected with Stalin. Now,' he says, 'the world will end. Who'll take his place? Whose word will be law now . . . ?'

"Who, me? No, I don't work now. When the war began, my Mishka was born. You yourself know, when there's a child in the house, all the fuss, one thing and another. . . . Only it hurts me very much—Misha doesn't get along with his father. As soon as his father says something, Mishka freezes up. He grinds his teeth, he even becomes menacing. I tell him, 'Mishenka, why are you insulting your father, he only wants the best for you!' And he answers me, 'Mama, he and I are different. He's blind. All his life he was blind. I can't be like that!' 'What do you want to do, Mishenka,' I say, 'change your papa? He's an old man, it's hard for him to learn new things. Life taught him to be like this.' And Misha says, 'No, Mama, I can't make him different. But just don't ask me to live his way. I hate it more and more.' What a sorrow. They'll never see eye-to-eye. One's old and one's young. They're stubborn—each has to prove his own way is right. The father turns pale and bangs on the table. 'In earlier times,' he says, 'you know what they'd do for such talk? Put you up against the wall!'

Comrade Shifrin!

And Mishka says, 'It's harder for you now! You'll have to shoot everyone!!' Why do they have to bring up these subjects. . . . It's not for us to figure out this business. . . . Here I've been gabbing with you, and the soup has boiled over. . . . But I read the book. . . . Not very carefully, but I read it. . . . "

The Fourth Reader

"IMMATURITY IS THE DEFECT of your generation. You become men too late. And often you stay boys forever. With you, one always feels unsure, for you're incapable of action. Of course, it's our fault. We ourselves created the conditions for you. . . . That's because we tried to hide our disappointments from you. Many things turned out not to our liking. I understand very well how your hero came into existence, of course I do. I remember how we used to sing: 'We're peaceful people, but our armored train . . . ,' 'Budyonny, call us bolder into battle . . . ,' 'The sated horses pound their hooves, We'll meet the enemy in Stalin's fashion. . . .'

"The sated horses pounded their hooves, but the enemy was already approaching Moscow. How could it all have happened? Imagine—we young, healthy lads lying in a trench. It's cold. We're hungry. . . . And behind every bush lurks a German. On the right—a German. On the left—the same. And in the sky. Especially in the sky. And he chops us up, the devil, flying low. And tanks. Cursed, grinding tanks, against which everything seems useless. And you have an 1891-vintage rifle. That's the way it is. And the worst thing is the uncertainty. Why are we retreating? Where's our air force?

Comrade Shifrin!

What's happened to our cannons? Where are we going? "Our platoon is all Muscovites. There we are in luck. Imagine—we're lying in the trench, shooting at shadows on the horizon, and suddenly—vzzz!—and Kolya Lopukhov is slammed against the ground. Vzzz!—and Mishka Rubinchik is dead. You bite your lip in rage and fill up with hate. Kill, kill them, like rats, like scorpions. And you're shooting, shooting, shooting into shadows on the horizon, until the lieutenant commands a retreat. Again, a retreat! God damn it, why retreat?! And we retreat once more, hastily throwing dirt on Kolya Lopukhov and Mishka Rubinchik.

"And then . . . then I saw German automatic rifles in front of me. *'Hände hoch!'* You know those phrases in the battle reports: 'In carrying out Operation N——, more than———thousand enemy soldiers and officers were captured!' Well, I was one of those '———thousand enemy soldiers and officers.' Only on the other side . . .

"They led us along the dusty roads near Moscow. The column was long and we were always getting new additions. We passed through the countryside. Children and old people stood by the fences, looking sternly and pityingly at our dirty, unshaven faces, our gray field jackets, gray as the dust of the road, which we stirred up with our bare feet. The Germans were jolly. They laughed and shot at those of us who couldn't walk any more or who lagged behind. . . . They purred their guttural songs and slapped us on the back. They were full and contented. *'Moskau— kaput!'* they said. *'Stalin—kaput! Russland—kaput!'* And I thought of my house near the Red Gates, and my mama who would die of grief when she found out that I was 'missing in action.' I imagined the Germans marching on Red Square, blowing up Lenin's mausoleum. . . . It was unbearable. . . .

"They lined us up, and some officer came over and

said in Russian, 'Officers, Bolsheviks, and Jews—step forward!' Everyone knew what would happen, and no one stepped out. The officer laughed and walked along the line, staring us in the eye. He no doubt thought he was an expert at physiognomy. From time to time he stopped and poked someone in the chest with a finger sheathed in black kidskin. He would poke someone and say, 'Jew' ... or 'Commissar' ... or 'Bolshevik.' ... The soldiers would drag that man from the line, and a moment later there would be a short blast of machine-gun fire from behind a wooden shed. ... He looked me in the eye for a very long time. Then he laughed and walked on.

"Banal, no? We've gotten used to such scenes. In the movies, in books ... But it really was like that. And I was eighteen years old! And I didn't want to die! The officer walked on, and I remained alive. There was only one thing I wanted to do—run away. Run away! We'd come to a bend, and bolting like a rabbit, I'd run into the woods, come what may. There we were, walking along the road, with the German guards smoking and lighting cigarettes for one another. Now! ... No, impossible! The column trudged on in silence, we didn't talk to one another: we didn't trust one another. Who is this ragged guy walking next to me? An animal's face ... Most likely a former kulak. He was probably waiting for the Germans like manna from heaven and surrendered in the first battle. Oh, the traitor! And who was I? I was also captured. Probably the guy with the animal face was thinking the same things about me. ...

"They interrogated us in an old, half-destroyed village school. The interrogation was conducted by that same officer in the black kid gloves.

"He said to me, 'Sit down. How can you be useful?'

" 'I can't,' I said.

" 'Such a young boy,' he said, 'and you're already looking for a bullet. You shouldn't be in such a hurry!'

Comrade Shifrin!

"He spoke Russian really well. He spoke so well that he seemed to be an actor dressed in a German uniform, who would say any minute, 'Okay, the show's over. Did I play my part well?'

"Later I did run away. I ran away from that column. I lay in a roadside ditch, and the ranks of captives closed over me. I picked just the right moment. It was at a turn. And when they had passed, I got up and ran into the woods. Funny, no? The Brothers Grimm. But that's how it was! Oh, my forest, my wonderful forest! My bitter freedom! Inside me, nothing but my hammering heart, and above me, the sky, the treetops; below me, leaves and grass. Grass! And there was no war. Just a man in the forest. And air. And no war . . .

"Eventually, I made my way to our troops. Twenty times I died, twenty times I dropped from hunger and fear, twenty times they could have caught me. But I made it to our troops. I just had to get there.

"I was interrogated by a counterintelligence officer from SMERSH. He tapped his cigarette case against the table. He had a weary face. When I told him what had happened, he looked at me closely. He looked me in the eye for a long time and said, 'You're lying, of course. Where should we send you now? . . . You don't fool us, we know everything. . . .'

"My God, why did he look so much like an actor in costume?

"I don't know why I brought all this up. It was so many years ago. Oh, yes, your book. . . . As I was saying —an immature generation. We were better prepared for life, but also terribly naive. We thought that life was like the newspaper headlines. And when we came up against it . . ."

197

The Fifth Reader

"I MISSED ONE very important detail in your story. You see, the barbed wire entangling the whole country divided it into two sections: the camp in which fifty million people rotted alive, and the camp in which the other two hundred million rotted alive. Our prison is on both sides of the barbed wire. The only difference is the living conditions. Essentially the prisoners are the same on both sides, and the overseers are the same on both sides. This is not even so awful, because it's obvious to everyone except blind men and fools; what *is* awful is that the prisoners don't want to get free—they want to become overseers! And that is the regime's main accomplishment.

"Your hero understood something, came to some conclusions. Only he didn't come to the simple and clear conclusion—to get out! Am I afraid to talk like this? Not any more. All my life I was afraid, and now I'm not. Because I know that I'm going to leave. I've got to get out of this country and its living death.

"You're all yelling, 'Give us freedom, give us back the right to criticize, free the market for production!' But think about it: how can a regime built on absolute, uncontrollable, bloody power give back to you what it

Comrade Shifrin!

took at the price of such unimaginable force? It never can! "I know, I know what you'll say: 'Then we must struggle against such a regime.' But look two steps further ahead. Dictators have never given up their power without a fight. And they won't now! But just for a moment, let's imagine that, God forbid, a revolution starts. Remember, this is Russia! Revolution in Russia is always a barbaric civil war. Have you forgotten what is was like back there in the twenties? First there will be the terror, annihilating the intellectuals, or their pitiful remains, and, of course, the Jews. Then, as the science of history teaches us, the people standing in the shadows will annihilate those who made this revolution, and, of course, the Jews. And then the next step: destruction and starvation. Because this future revolution will be directed at smashing the universally hated old apparatus. And who can make a new one? Who knows how to work? And here is the regime's second tremendous accomplishment: they've destroyed human initiative and the ability to work in a 'pre-socialist' society.

"Okay, so you've chased out the tyrants and dictators and want to open your bakery shop. Any ordinary man in the West and in the East, too, will tell me now, 'So I'll open it!' But a Russian, a Soviet man, can't say that. How can I open a bakery? Who'll give me flour, and who'll pay the salespeople, and who'll give me money? And who'll give me . . . ? Give!? This Soviet man has an atrophied sense of 'I myself,' he has a conditioned reflex to the words 'they'll give.' But there will *be* no one to give! Yes, I understand, *they* will help! They'll give! See, again it's 'they'll give.' But what will they give? Money. And what about experience, and work habits, and ability, and desire, and a guarantee that it won't happen all over again? . . . And will they also 'give' people who are able to create? And what if they refuse to give? Why? Well, imagine the point of view of the ones who will 'give.' Russia is an enormous country of many millions —with inexhaustible resources. If you feed her, clothe her, give her an idea of economic freedom, et cetera, et cetera—she will become a great and wealthy power, an invincible competitor in the world market. And who benefits from this? So, will they 'give,' or won't they? And if they won't? Our generation will experience a fate that even the poor contemporaries of Lenin's 'war communism' and Stalin's 'collectivization' didn't dream of.

"But let's be more realistic. Let's look at the recent past. Let's look at China. Doesn't your hair stand on end when you imagine the future battle with our eastern 'friend'? Don't you feel mortal terror at just the thought that for a nameless Hill Number Six the opposing forces will tear each other apart, both under red flags, both wearing red stars on their helmets, and both yelling in different languages the identical incantations of doomed men—for instance, 'Glory to Comrade Lenin!' Can you see yourself in the attackers' ranks, or, better said, in the retreating ranks? Myself, I cannot. I don't want to die there, near the Amur River, with this motto on my lips. I don't want to be responsible for the crimes of insane leaders. I have to get out!

"Let's come back down, down to our sinful earth. I work. I have a very good job and a perfectly adequate salary. I'm a competent specialist. I made a mistake, though, you see, I made a mistake in college. In my time, they didn't accept me for study in the field where I had a real vocation (like your hero, of course, but who's not like him?), and so I've done the wrong work all my life. And I have absolutely no chance to change my life and my profession. None! And all my life until old age and death I'll be in the wrong job. I don't want to do it any more. I can't. I want to live differently. A man changes with age, doesn't he? Habits change, and ideas, and one's way of life, and weltanschauung. A man

Comrade Shifrin!

is different at different ages. Some Japanese once said that during his life a man should change his name several times, because what he says when he's twenty is completely different from what he thinks when he's forty, and, of course, not what he assumes when he's sixty. But we can't do that! We're assigned to our apartments, our city, our nationality, our work, our thoughts, and our actions from the moment we're born. We're assigned, we're constructed, like machines, long before our birth. We 'must'! We have a perpetually unpaid 'debt'! All our lives the government says only two things to us: 'you must' and 'you mustn't.'
" 'You must, Vasya! You must do it this way.'
" 'No, Vasya, you mustn't!'
"All our lives like that! From the cradle. And what lies ahead? Ahead life is clear, clear to madness. With always exactly the same schedule: to work, home from work, television, sometimes the movies, in summer a vacation with your wife to the south to some flea-bag hotel for three rubles a day, then back to work, where it's forbidden to express or carry out even one fresh idea. Then a pension and the terrible, piddling job at the shop near your house or the numbing game of dominoes with other sour, useless old men like yourself, thrown overboard from even such a wretched life as ours. Then the crematorium, with its employees' hurried whisper: 'Faster, faster, comrades, you're not the only ones here, there are others waiting . . .'
"We've turned into gods who know their own future. What could be more boring than that! Only twenty years until my pension. I don't want to know my future ahead of time! I want to create it myself! I have to get out. When I leave here, I'll begin all over again. I'll outwit time, be twenty again. And I'll begin studying again. I'll learn how to live. And I want to save my children! I want it to be easier for them.
"Where should I go? But that's another question. The

main issue is what am I leaving? Am I not afraid? Sure, I'm afraid! Everything's different over there. Most important, the language is strange. How terrible to lose your language, God, how frightening! That soft Moscow *'shto'* and the chiseled Leningrad *'chto,'* and the Volga *'o'* and the Siberian *'tso,'* and a whole world of idioms, slang, obscenities, inferred meanings, jokes, and aphorisms that exist only in Russian. And all our linguistic license, that word play, when you understand the language of parody and style and know its sources and reasons for being. And your Russian thoughts, your Russian thoughts—what will you do with them, who will you tell them to? But all the same, one must get out. I must leave! Not what's dear to me, what's my own, what I've gotten used to, what I love, what I live on— but I must leave this deadening, destructive, uncompassionate and immoral lawlessness!

"Lawlessness in the guise of law. A law with retroactive force. Just think, suppose today I did something that is considered against the law. I know that my infringement, my crime, should get me a year in prison, let's say. So they try me. And then someone telephones the judge in the courtroom and says that there's a new law now by which the crime I committed must get, say, ten years in prison. Or the punishment is hanging! As they say, trust him, but shoot him just to be sure! And the judge hangs up the phone and me at the same time! They have no old law protecting me from the new one! And there is no judge or lawyer who could protect me from that! Because the judge, and the lawyer, and the prosecutor, and the investigator, and the guard, and the 'people's juror'—all of them protect not the law, but one man who unites in one person the court, the law, and the power of the state. . . .

"Probably some ordinary Westerner, spoiled by his right to choose and use, will exclaim with vehemence, 'My God, if those Russians live like that, why do they

Comrade Shifrin!

stand for it? They should get together and change such a society! After all, there are two hundred and fifty million of them!'
" 'You silly fool,' I'd say to such a person, 'you don't understand anything. That's impossible in a government where everything is turned upside down. Once,' I'd say to him, 'someone asked the famous director and actor N. P. Akimov, now deceased, "Nikolai Pavlovich! You're a talented man. Why don't you put on a really good play in your theater?" He answered, "And who'd let me put on such a play?" How can you work well in a country where the players are chosen by a method the reverse of natural selection?'
" 'Think,' I'd say, 'just think about it. The reverse of natural selection! Everything that should die off is in power! Everything that by all laws of evolution is dead—lives! Everything vital is dead! Just think about that . . .'
"One must get out! It has always been so. There have been other exoduses. People left for happiness and because of unhappiness. They left with hope and despair. In search of the promised land and lost times. An exodus from a country where the intellectuals are equated with the Jews, the Jews are equated with the peasants, the peasants are equated with the workers, the workers are equated with slaves, slaves are equated with prisoners, prisoners are equated with animals, and animals are equated with people! We're all equal! And if this is the equality that the best human minds have dreamed about—I wish to be excused, but I don't want to participate in such equality! It makes me sick! I want a simple order of things, where we're all equal before the law: the sailor, the carpenter, the blacksmith, the reaper, and the piper! I don't want to dread tomorrow—a tomorrow of long knives and atomic wars between two tentacles of one octopus.

Here's to Your Health,

"I must leave! And if anyone says that this is desertion, I'll answer that it is escape from prison!

"So that's why it seems to me that you didn't adequately show the country 'on the other side' of the barbed wire. By the way, you're not a propagandist, a politician, are you? You just 'painted life,' right? Well, that's all right, that's needed, too."